infinity

infinity

ellen curtis
matthew ledrew

Published in Canada by Engen Books, St. John's, NL.

Library and Archives Canada Cataloguing in Publication data is available upon request.

ISBN-13: 978-1-989473-43-6

Distributed by:
Engen Books
www.engenbooks.com
submissions@engenbooks.com

First mass market paperback printing: October 2010

Cover Image: Ellen Curtis

To our friend
Amanda Labonté
and for Connor Reilly.

PROLOGUE

Northton, Idaho

Mary Crane smiled as she lay on her bed, her long blonde hair falling over her. She opened up the photo album she'd pulled from a long library of photo albums, poring over pictures of herself and her boyfriend at the county fair three months ago.

She was pretty. It seemed like all seventeen year old girls were pretty in some way or another, but she was exceptionally so. Her hair hadn't been cut in nearly ten years except for occasional trims, and she was meticulous about keeping it healthy. It had a shine to it that made it seem like a trail of pixie dust was following her wherever she went, drawing the attention of everyone she passed. She didn't wear brand names, preferring to make her own clothes with the same old-fashioned sewing machine her mother had used at her age. There had been a few mishaps during the first few years of this... failed experiments that had resulted in jeering from her peers and the occasional hole ripped in awkward areas, but for the most part it had been fine and now she'd become quite the seamstress;

even making a few dollars around prom season making dresses for the senior girls.

And she loved showing them off for her boyfriend.

She was never sure if he was actually interested or just being supportive, but he would wait in her living room for hours as she tried on creation after creation and walked out for him, even offering helpful suggestions such as the positioning of a hem or the colour of an accessory. More than once she'd marvelled at how lucky she was to have such a caring, considerate man.

A necklace was clasped at her throat, a present that he'd given her. It was simple spun twine holding a perfectly smooth stone in the shape of a teardrop between her breasts. She'd found it on a trip to the beach last summer and given it to him. He'd given it back a week later, polished to a near mirror shine and placed into a metal backing he'd made by melting down his junior ring. It had rarely left her person since, only removed in situations where it could get lost or damaged.

She smiled again, finding a picture of them both with cotton-candy smiles, her mouth pushing up her freckly cheeks and making her face heart-shaped. She closed the album again, placing it back on her shelf with the others in the right space.

Her reflection in her vanity caught her eye and she stepped over to it, flicking a switch on its side that made five bright lights spotlight her. She examined herself a moment, swishing her mouth back and forth contemplatively. Clicking her tongue against the roof of her mouth, she picked up her brush, dabbed on a healthy slab of foundation and began to apply it.

A cool draft came in through the window next to her, blowing her curtains about and showering her with fresh air. She took it in deeply, the scent of the pine from outside a welcome one. Glancing outside, her blueish-green eyes watched as the evergreen trees swayed in the moonlight. Their branches seemed to make the faces of old men, chattering to each other in their secret tree-language, creaking the way her grandfather's rocking chair always had.

There were shrubs beneath them that were dense with foliage in all but one place, a trail worn after decades of use. It seemed a fact of life in rural communities that if you were under the age of twenty, you were going to invent paths to get to where you needed to go. Would in fact take any way, except the actual street.

The path itself was always shadowed, no matter what the time of day. But at night, like now, it was pitch black. There could be a hundred people secluded under the howling arms of evergreen and you'd never see them scampering about. It was a thought that usually led her to leave her blinds closed, but it was too nice a night to do that.

Tonight a man was on the trail, as quiet as a mouse except for heavy, hard breaths. He was crouching down on one knee to see under the branches and into her window, watching as she finished with her foundation and started to brush those long, luscious locks of hair. He smiled, revealing a long row of jagged and gray teeth. His eyes were pupil-less but could see perfectly; dancing over her from the top of her head right down to her flannel pink pajamas.

He reached up and scratched his long slender face,

making an odd scraping sound with nails that were short but thick. They were almost a full millimetre each, and had turned the sickly yellow of mushed peas.

Inside, Mary stood up and started to unbutton her pajamas, stepping out of the window's view.

He smiled.

CHAPTER 01

Port Haven, California

Abigail Louise Fisher stared out at the watery darkness, the silver moon reflecting in the almost still waves. The sky was noticeably darker than it had been mere hours ago when she had first assumed her current position, leaning against the rail.

She wished she could be as still as the waves, but inside her own waves were crashing.

At that moment, she felt older than she ever had. At twenty-two, she had seen more than most people would in a lifetime. A gloom hung over her that she could not shake, clinging to her like morning fog.

Finally summoning up the courage to move, she turned to head back indoors and to the shelter of a dreamless sleep. Five steps got her to the door, another got her inside, and twelve more got her to her bed. She kicked off her shoes and snuggled under the covers, not realizing how cold she had been until she was warm again.

She stared at the ceiling. There were spots in front of her eyes, her body's way of telling her that she was tired, yet she still didn't sleep.

It wasn't until the sun crept in through the shades that she closed her eyes, but only briefly. Less than ten minutes later, a loud hammering began on her door.

"I'm up! I'm up!" she called, bringing both hands to her face.

"Abby!" The person outside growled, continuing to knock fiercely.

"I'm up!" she screamed, then waited until the knocking stopped before groaning and rolling out of the covers. She sat on the edge of her bed and sighed, staring at the plush floor in front of her and waiting for the haze to work its way out of her vision.

"At least it's better than the alternative," she said under her breath, forcing herself to get up.

She dressed quickly, shirking off the camisole and boxers she had worn to bed and pulling on a tee-shirt and denim overalls. She scrunched her auburn hair into a pigtail and glanced around the small room, made sure nothing was out of place, then walked swiftly out her bedroom door.

The hallway wound itself in a long, sweeping circuit around the coed dorm of the school. The walls were forest green with gold trim (at least in this section), and coloured lines on the wall showed newcomers which way to go to make it to the bathrooms, mess hall, gym, and other such amenities. Students walked this way and that, in one door and out the other, somehow not bumping into each other even though nobody seemed to be watching where they were going. It was this quirk of the student body that had taken Abby the longest to get used to, but she was finally beginning to.

Whoever had knocked on her door was gone now, moved on to wake the next student. She rubbed her temples, adjusting as the light hit her eyes, and made her way through the gaggle of students into the common room.

From the outside looking in the common room seemed mundane enough, with a circle of leather chairs all arranged around a small, round coffee table made of glass. It was only when she stepped in that she saw how high the ceilings were, each of them lined with bookcases that were packed solid with every title imaginable; from Hamlet to Holmes, Herodotus to Stevenson.

Sitting back in the chair furthest to the left with his feet up on the table, was Theo Flaherty. He had loosely cut light hair and a clean shaven face. He pretended to read the morning paper as she approached. When she got close, he bent back the edge of the paper enough to see her.

"You're looking perky this morning, sweetheart," he said, smiling as he looked up.

"Hello to you too, Mr. Flaherty," she droned, running her fingers through her hair. "Sarcasm is not appreciated this early in the morning."

"Neither is being awake, but that's what we signed up for, isn't it?" he laughed, tossing the paper onto the table and jumping to his feet.

"I don't recall signing up at all, actually," Abby mumbled to herself, her tone dull and exasperated. She turned and walked to the other side of the common room, bumping her way through an open door and into the mess hall.

infinity

Theo came up behind her, leaned over and hugged her warmly. "Who does?"

The duo shuffled over to the breakfast line. Theo grabbed the trays, plates and utensils for the both of them.

"Nothing like rehydrated eggs in an omelette, eh?" he winked.

"Oh, suck it up," Abby rolled her eyes, a smile creeping into the corners of her mouth.

Port Haven Institute was probably one of the most beautiful places Abby had ever been. Lush forest surroundings, a secluded and untouched oceanfront view, large windows and larger facilities that offered occupants the most for their time. The studios, recording halls, galleries, and fitness centers were all fully equipped, spacious and bold.

The scenery and residents were more than inspiring, yet she remained uninspired. Hardly anything excited her anymore.

Jasper Hemmingway. That had been what had broken the camels back. He had been the perfect boyfriend and best of best friends to her, yet all that could be overshadowed easily. He had been the best thing in her life, yet he had scarred her in the worst ways.

That was how it went, after all, when you see someone you love die.

He was the only part of her life at peace. His death was the least of her worries though, in a long string of events going from bad to worse.

One bright light had crept into her life since she came to Port Haven, and he was doing his best to keep Abby from drowning.

Theo Flaherty had been at Port Haven for less than two months when the petite, frail looking girl had arrived in the lobby looking lost and confused. He had known then that there was more going on under her timid surface, but as he had gotten to know her, he was horrified by the secrets that lurked beneath...

...secrets even she didn't know.

He had sworn not to tell her, he wouldn't be the one to hurt her even more. If anything, he would make sure she grew stronger, surer... so that over time she could uncover the secrets for herself, and live to tell the tale.

The pair ate in silence, stowed their dishes in the dirty bin, and exited the common room. Abby pulled her hair out of the ponytail ring absent mindedly as the pair navigated the halls, heading for the lobby.

"Deidre won't mind if we're a bit late will she? I have something to show you," Theo asked, praying she wouldn't read too much into what he'd said. She had a habit of doing that.

"She shouldn't have a problem with you being late," she frowned. "You're her favorite, and all the teachers know enough to let me be. Where are we headed anyway?"

Theo smiled. "Art Studio 11."

CHAPTER 02

Salt Lake City, Utah

"You seen the story in this weeks Star?" Victor smirked into his cell phone, slapping the rolled up newspaper onto the hood of his car. He stopped, closed his eyes for a moment and sighed, then let a smile spread slowly over his face. "No, not the Elvis story. The next page... I'm sure that would be great, but it's not. Yeah, I'm fairly certain he isn't one. Will you turn the page already?"

He grabbed the styrofoam cup off the roof of the beaten-up El Dorado he was driving, pushing back the long, straggly blonde hair from either side of his face as he took a sip from it. The scalding hot coffee burned his tongue but he didn't recoil away, and instead chugged it back faster. When he brought the cup away again, thick globs of foam stuck to the yellow scruff that covered his upper lip and chin.

"I know," he said finally, putting the cup back onto the roof carefully before opening up the newspaper with a flick of his wrist. "Kid's barely twenty-one, wins the county poker championship last month. Three large. Two weeks ago, sets the county record for the amount won on a single bet at the track. Fifteen thousand... I know, yeah, it's a long shot... I know. But I got a feeling about this kid. I think he's gonna be one of ours... anyway, friggin' tabloid says the kid got the goods from the future... like that damn sports Almanac from that time-travel movie... no, not the first one. The one that sucked. Yeah. No, no I don't think it's anything like that. M'thinkin it's something a little closer to home."

He stopped talking, stepping back a pace as he watched a tall young man with long hay-coloured hair drawn into a ponytail step out of the entrance of the nearby apartment building. He did not bother to look both ways before crossing the busy city street, hands shoved in his pockets and headphones blaring in either ear.

"And a hell of a lot scarier," Victor finished, taking another slurp of his coffee and curling up his face, pouring it out onto the sidewalk. "Miss you, too. We'll talk soon. Out."

He hung up the phone with one finger and shoved it back down into the breast pocket of the flannel shirt he wore loosely over his box-like frame, still watching the young man with the headphones as he did.

"That'll be forty-two ninety-five," the clerk said, holding her petite hand out in front of her without so much as making eye contact with the person she was serving.

The customer was an older woman with ghostly white hair and a pink wool sweater draped over her shoulders gingerly. She had on sunglasses that took up over half her face, with lime green rims and dark reflective lenses. She pulled her purse out of her handbag, grabbing each side of the clasp and bracing herself for exertion. After a moment she paused, turning slowly to look over her shoulder.

A few feet away, a man with a shoulder-length blonde ponytail and a vacant stare ogled a display for Ovaltine. His head swayed back and forth slightly to the beat of the heavy metal music that blared over his headphones. It was so loud that everyone in proximity could hear it as clearly as if it had been over a stereo speaker.

The woman eyed him for a moment, then turned back to the cashier and opened her purse, withdrawing a folded fifty dollar bill and placing it in her hand.

The younger girl took it quickly, turning slightly and pressing the 'SALE' button on the register as if she'd just painted the final stroke to a masterful work of art. The cash drawer opened with a delightful -bing!- followed by a series of mechanical whirs as she slid the fifty into its proper slot, then snapped out three bills and some change before pushing the drawer shut with her hip. "That's seven-oh-five your change. Is there anything else I can do to help you?"

She glanced over her shoulder again before grabbing up her bags and leaving without a word.

The man with the ponytail watched her from the corner, pretending to examine a flyer, his eyes following her until she went through the automatic doors and disappeared out into the street. He put the flyer down immediately and began to walk toward where she had been, stopping at the register and cocking his head toward the cashier with the short brunette hair. "The hell's her problem?"

"I actually think it was you, Chad." She smiled and rolled her eyes as she brushed some of the dust off the counter and into the palm of her hand, then sprinkled it into the garbage can at her feet.

"Me?" Chad asked, raising an eyebrow as he pulled each headphone out of his ear by its cord. "What'd I do?"

"You looked a little creepy. Over there, in the corner, watching her like a hawk."

"Was waiting for her to leave."

"Yeah, she got that," she laughed, holding her hand up to her nose as she did.

He scuffed his feet, winding the thin headphone cords around his index finger until they were coiled in a neat little ball, then shoved them into his jacket pocket. He looked at her for a long moment, then let a smile slowly grow along the right side of his face.

She smiled too, straightening her green apron and laughing a little at him.

"How was she?" he asked finally, leaning in and looking around the other side of the counter.

"She was great," she said, nodding and bobbing up and down on her heels. Even at the highest point in the motion, when she was on the tips of her toes, she only came up to his shoulder. "She made it almost the whole way through Friday the Thirteenth parts one and two, and now she's stocking the beer cooler."

He shot her a look.

"Ha," she forced, tapping him on the arm. "Kidding. We bonded, it was cool."

"Good. Where is she?"

Karen leaned over the cash and pressed a small green button just to one side of it. A loud tone rang out all over the store and the next time she spoke it echoed an instant later over the store's speakers. "Koy, you're needed at the front desk. Koy to the front desk."

There was a hard smack as something dropped in the aisles and then rolled, followed by a succession of quick steps.

Chad winced as the rolling came to an abrupt halt, then smiled at Karen. "Could've been worse."

She giggled at him, leaning over the counter to watch the ends of the aisles.

A tiny, plump little girl with wispy brunette hair and a cheeky smile stepped out from between the shelves. She was tall for three and had orange hand prints on either side of her shirt from the Cheesies she'd been given earlier. She was in view only an instant when her eyes went to Chad and lit up instantly, her smile brightening as she ran toward him with arms outstretched. "Tad!"

He grinned, kneeling to her level and scooping her up into his arms, planting a firm kiss on her cheek. "Hey sweetie, what'd you do today?"

"I help Kar with the paper, over dare," she said, then pointed to a large stack of paper on one of the shelves, just in case he didn't know.

"Yeah?"

"Yeah. And den, we coloured in the big book and it was really really good and Kar sayed that I was taking hers and I said 'no Kar, is mine'."

"Yeah?"

"Yeah. And then I danced for Kar and add some worms

and payed with my toys."

Chad turned from Koy to Karen and raised an eyebrow. "She danced for you?"

Karen smiled. "Around an hour ago she just asked me to record her with my cell phone and started dancing. She was making up her own moves and her own words, then she'd ask me to play it back for her. I've got about ten videos on my phone of her now."

"I'm gonna wanna see those," he laughed, rubbing noses with Koy. She giggled.

"I'll upload them the next chance I get."

He put Koy back down. "Go get your jacket," he smiled, patting her on the back. She grinned and ran around the side of the front desk to where her pink plastic jacket had been laid. He couldn't help but chuckle when he watched her run, still uncertain sometimes on her feet.

Karen beamed at him, blushing a little when he turned back to her. "Same time tomorrow?"

"Yeah." He scuffed his feet, scratching the back of his head. "Actually, I might need you before then."

"Before tomorrow morning?"

He avoided eye contact again, leaning over the counter to see what Koy was doing.

She huffed, jutting one hand into her hip apprehensively. "You're not going there again tonight, are you?"

He didn't answer, but finally looked at her again, his face flushed and filled with that hot, livid shame that men could usually only feel when confronted by their mother. It lasted only a moment until Koy came back out from around the corner, causing the smile to return to his face. It was slightly less genuine now though.

"You said you wouldn't go anymore," she continued. She seemed to get more and more agitated the more
she spoke on the subject. "You promised. You swore you
wouldn't."

"I need the money," he said sheepishly, helping Koy
zip up her jacket.

"Then you should get a real job."

He scoffed. "Doing what? Working cash? Taking
calls?"

She took a step back, appearing hurt.

"Not that there's anything wrong with it... I just
couldn't do it. I'm not cut out for that kind of work. It's
not that the job's bad, it's that it just doesn't fit me. You
put me behind a counter or at a desk, I start to go crazy. I
need... more, Karen."

"What you need is to swallow your goddamn pride,"
she said, finally losing her patience. "You're going to get
yourself killed."

"Hey," he urged, motioning down at Koy. "Watch
it."

"Sorry," she frowned, grabbing a cloth and starting
to run it across the glass lotto display, polishing until the
grease from peoples fingers finally started to wear away.

He frowned, knowing full well that this meant the
conversation was over. Pressing it further would only
result in an argument that wouldn't serve any purpose
except to make the both of them mad. He looked down at
Koy, who smiled back up at him with a mouth full of tiny
round teeth, then pressed her finger to the side of her nose
and laughed. He had no idea what that was supposed to
mean, it was just one of those things she'd picked up a few

months ago and seemed to think was very funny.

And it was.

He laughed along with her and picked her up, planting another kiss on her cheek. "Where do you want to eat today?"

She looked thoughtful for a moment, her eyes tilting upward as she tapped her chin contemplatively with one finger. He didn't think she had any trouble deciding at all, merely that somewhere she'd gotten it in her head that that was what people did before they made any decision, no matter how mundane or easy. He didn't bother correcting her on it, mainly because it was unbelievably cute. "Pizza," she said finally.

"Pizza?" he rebuked in a comical, over exaggerated fashion that made her laugh. "Pizza isn't breakfast food! You had pizza for lunch yesterday!"

"Pizza."

"If we get pizza, we're getting what I want on it."

"Cheese?"

"No, not cheese! Worms and snails feet!"

She scrunched up her face and recoiled slightly, waiting to see if he was joking. When he didn't retract it, she spoke in a low voice. "I don' want pizza."

He smiled. "Do you wanna go to Janelle's Place over across the way? You love their breakfast, and you know Suzie there always gives you a toy when you come in 'cause you're her special girl."

She put that contemplative look on her face again, then nodded happily.

"Yeah?"

"Yeah!"

"Okay," he laughed, hoisting her up into a sturdy position to prepare for the walk to Janelle's. He turned back to Karen, still wiping off the counter top. He frowned as she continued to ignore him for a moment, then finally stopped and turned to Koy, smiling.

"I'll see you later, alligator!" she smiled, reaching and out and tickling Koy's cheek.

Koy laughed. "Imalyle crocdiele!"

She laughed. It was a wonderful sound. After it died off she turned back to Chad. She didn't speak for a moment, regarding him with a suspicious smile.

"So..." he drawled, rapping his fingers along the counter. "... around eight?"

She tried her best to stay mad, but a thin smile spread across her lips despite her best intentions. "You're a lucky man, Chad Matthews."

"Let's hope," he smiled, giving her a small salute before heading toward the door. "Thanks again. I owe you big time."

"Yes," she called after him, even as he was going out the door. "You do!"

Port Haven, California

Theo pushed open the large wooden entry doors, holding them open so Abby could slink out behind him. The pair turned away from the long, winding dirt driveway toward a narrower path shrouded by trees and shrubs.

He pushed away the low hanging branches and held them so that Abby could pass. She trod along slowly, not really wanting to see what he had to show her. His excitement was contagious, but she found it too painful to smile.

Finally, they reached Art Studio 11 and he pulled the small screen door open. Abby walked into the little cabin, lit from the east with floor to ceiling windows.

Inside were several large canvases in varying stages of completion. One was rather large and was almost completely taken up by the image of an apple, ripe on one side but rotting on the other. Another was of a wolf baying at the moon, the sickly glow of twilight gathering around it. The third... was of a woman.

He crept in behind her and put his arms around Abby's waist. "Which one do you think I did?"

Abby snuggled into his embrace, his body still warm from the sunshine. She pointed toward the large canvas of the woman that looked complete. "That one?"

He smiled.

The piece was composed mainly of hued pinks and reds, swirling to form a woman's figure. Large gold and green wings sprung from her back, and her hair flowed out in a rusty red wave. She seemed to explode from the page.

"What do you think of her?" he asked, his voice as quiet as a whisper.

"She's beautiful," she said, breathless. "So full of life."

Theo blushed.

"She looks so real. Why didn't you tell me you were working on this? Have you shown this to any of the professors yet?"

"Nobody's seen this but you and I... and the five other

people who use this room. I'm going to show Grayson this afternoon. I wanted it to be a surprise."

"How long have you been working on this?" she asked, turning to look over her shoulder at him.

"Since the day you got here."

Salt Lake City, Utah

Koy took a bite of her burger.

Chad laughed, so hard that he almost squirted root beer out of his nose.

There was nothing particularly humorous about the way she did it. None of the dressings were falling out and she didn't have a funny look on her face or anything. It was simply the proportion of the burger to her head that made it amusing. She was holding it for dear life with both hands, her chubby fingers sinking into the bread, opening her mouth as wide as she could before diving toward the patty. Even after all that effort, she still only managed to take a chunk the size of his thumb.

She stopped eating, cocking one eyebrow at him and giving him a very serious look.

He tried to stop laughing, pursing his lips tightly. Still, one or two giggling spurts came out, and she looked horribly offended. "I'm sorry, Koy," he offered sympathetically.

She frowned, staring at him from over her bun, then picked up a french fry and slathered it with ketchup before putting it in her mouth.

He smiled, then glanced over her shoulder at Suzie as she picked up dishes off a far table. She huffed and poked a curly strand of hair into her scrunchie forcefully. There was a thin layer of sweat over her forehead, and her cheeks were red from the heat of the kitchen, although it was relatively cool out here in the main dining area. She was wearing a yellow blouse and black skirt beneath her apron, all of which clung to her as though it were concerned about flying away.

She cast a glance his way and forced a smile, looking him up and down.

He grinned back, winking at her.

The restaurant itself was nothing special. There was one just like it every neighbourhood in America. Everything was painted and decorated in earth tones: mauves and deep, deep browns. On the walls, just above every booth and table, was a black-and-white picture of something oddly clever, like a fire hydrant shooting water into a waiting child's chest or a clown standing on a street corner and being ignored by men in suits walking to and from work.

Koy burped, then took another sip of her soda. It drew his attention back to her for a moment, and he smiled. She smiled back, beaming giddily and then taking some more of her drink.

When he turned back to where Suzie had been standing she was gone, now giving him a clear view of the table she had been serving.

There was a man sitting at the table alone, a small cup of coffee idling steam beside him. He looked tall and had long, blonde hair very similar to his own, although a little better kept. He had a scruffy goatee that hid the corners of his mouth, making it hard to tell if he was smiling or frowning without the expression being exaggerated... and he didn't seem like the sort of man that was prone to exaggerated displays of emotion. The shirt he was wearing was tight black corduroy, and left little to the imagination when it came to the man's strength. He didn't look like there was an ounce of fat on him.

He was staring right at Chad.

There's a social contract that dictates that you don't stare at people in general, especially strangers. If for some reason you catch yourself staring at someone, be it because you were simply lost in thought or that you were genuinely interested in them, this contract states that you turn away immediately a) once you realize that you're staring or b) once the opposing party makes direct eye-contact with you, thus either breaking you out of your trance or catching you in your adolescent fantasy and making you turn away in shame.

This man did neither.

He continued to stare at Chad, his face devoid of all emotion. At first he didn't move at all, then slowly reached over and picked up his coffee and brought it to his lips, taking a sip.

Suzie walked over to Chad's table, stopping and forcing a smile across her face. Koy looked up at her and hummed excitedly. She smiled back, rustling her hair. "How's your burger, sweetie?"

Koy gave an enthusiastic thumbs up.

"You need any more pop?"

She turned to examine her half-empty glass, then shook her head so vigorously that her hair whipped from side to side.

She laughed, then turned her attention to Chad. "What about you? How were your eggs?"

"Good," he said, patting his stomach. "As usual. How've you been?"

"Pretty good. Claire came over last night and we went downtown... forgot to eat something before going and got smashed on tequila shooters. No hangover, but I'll think I'll be working overtime for a month to pay for that one night."

"Crappy."

"Yeah," she shrugged, reaching over and filling up his coffee. "How about you?"

"Top of the world," he said dryly, lifting his mug and giving her a small cheers before taking a sip. "So I can assume you're going to be working late tonight?"

She gave him a sideways glance, then smirked. "Should be here right until close."

"Hn," he said, nibbling at the remains of his eggs again. "Maybe I'll drop by if I'm done early tonight. See if you want any company."

She eyed him again for a moment. "Okay, sure. Maybe."

"Too?" Koy chimed, smiling from Chad to Suzie.

"Not this time, sweetie. Tomorrow, though," Chad laughed, reaching out and wiping some ketchup from the side of her face. When he did he couldn't help but glance over her shoulder again at the man on the other side of the restaurant.

He was still looking their way. Not staring exactly, just watching... the same way someone would watch a television show that they had a passing interest in.

Chad frowned, looking back to Suzie. "Who's that guy?" he asked, not motioning at all toward him and hoping that the direction of his vision would be enough.

She glanced over her shoulder and pretended to look across the entire restaurant, then turned back. "Not sure. He's not a regular... he's nice enough. Been sitting there for about an a hour. Doesn't talk much, but he's polite. 'Thank you' this and 'please' that."

"Hmm."

"Why? You know him?"

Chad paused a moment, then turned back to his plate. "Never saw him before in my life."

Koy looked at him for a moment as if trying to figure him out, then seemed to dismiss whatever she'd been thinking and reached for her glass.

"Be careful," Chad warned, pointing at her. "That's a big-girl cup, not a sippy cup... okay?"

She hesitated, then nodded, bringing the glass to her mouth and carefully tipping it up until the soda touched her lips and then slurped back loudly. She took several mouthfuls before putting the glass back down happily.

"Good girl!" he beamed. Suzie put down her coffee pot and clapped several times.

Koy beamed with excitement, leaning forward and humming with delight. An excited look on her face, she grabbed the glass again and took another gulp, knocking it back in a hurry.

Root Beer splashed from the glass in a tiny tidal wave, sloshing all over her face and into her eyes, hair, and all over her shirt. She closed her eyes tight and dropped the glass to her side, coughing several times in shock as Chad and Suzie rushed forward to help, grabbing a handful of paper towels each.

"Sweetie, are you okay?" Suzie asked, trying to get the sticky soda out of her hair.

Chad wiped her face wordlessly, sighing once as he discarded a soaked napkin.

After a moment she opened her eyes, which had welled up with tears, and looked from one to the other, then down at her now soaked burger and fries. She was silent for a moment, then her tiny body shook as she let out a sob. Then another. By the time the third one came, she had started to cry and was holding out her arms to Chad.

"Oh, Koy..." he soothed, picking her up and holding her to his shoulder. She pushed her head into the nape of his neck and continued to sob, soaking his shirt with her own in the process. He didn't mind.

Most of the people in the diner turned and looked. A few made sympathetic clucks or 'oos' and 'ahhs'.

From the back, one person chuckled softly.

Chad looked up to see who it was, although he already knew. It was the blonde neo-hippie, still sipping his coffee and now clearly smiling. Chad continued to bob Koy up and down, throwing the man a glance that was meant to say 'shut- the- fuck- up- and- close- the- door- when- you- leave'.

"Are you sad about your burger, honey?" Suzie asked, rubbing Koy's back. "Are you? I'll get Trevor to make you another burger, okay?" She made eye contact with Chad to make sure this was acceptable. He nodded once in simultaneous agreement and thanks, then went right back to bobbing Koy and making soothing sounds as she disappeared into the kitchen.

"It's okay, sweetie," he repeated, running his fingers through her hair. She wasn't really crying now, but the sobbing continued. "It's okay. It's only a bit of pop, we'll get you some more. And we'll stop into WalMart on the way home to make sure you don't get cold. It's okay. It's ooookay."

"She's not upset about the soda," the man in the back said in a matter-of-fact tone, laying down his coffee and standing up. "She's embarrassed. She liked that you were proud of her for drinking out of the cup and then she spilled it. She's embarrassed."

"That a fact?" Chad scoffed, looking the man up and down.

"It is," he said, bending over now to look Koy in the eye. "It's going to be okay. Happens to the best of us."

Chad turned her away, glaring at the man. "You mind?"

He stopped, rising back to stand ramrod straight. He seemed to study Chad for a moment, then gave the briefest hint of a smile from beneath his scruff. "Of course. I was just on my way to pay my tab."

Chad watched him stroll over to the counter and leave a twenty on it. He did not wait for Suzie to come back and give him change, just turned on his heels with military precision and walked to the exit.

Suzie came back from the kitchen, carrying a fresh burger platter in one hand and more paper towels in the other. "How is she?"

He leaned back and pulled her forward to see her face. Her eyes weren't puffy and she'd stopped crying and sobbing. She looked sad though, and only made eye contact with him tentatively.

"She's fine," he said, bending over and carefully placing her back into her seat. "I think she was just embarrassed."

∞

Port Haven, California

Hand in hand, Theo and Abby walked toward Professor Deidre's sparring field.

The fencing teacher was a tall, wiry woman with a mane of curly violet hair and a quick wit. Theo was her most prized student. He was the only one who would joust with Abby, for what she lacked in skill she made up for in fury. She was vicious, perhaps owing to her bottled rage and the rest to her naturally competitive spirit. She would do what it took to win, even if it meant bending the rules. Jousting was the only place where she allowed herself that.

The duo followed a wooden fence until they came to an archway, ducked inside and entered a wide grassy field. In its center was a large, dirt circle that was currently occupied by a dozen or more students.

They were paired off and began sparring with one another, kicking up dust with each elaborate move they made. Walking through their midst was Professor Deidre, navigating her way through the barrage of swords and thrusts as calmly as a normal woman would have strolled through the park on a spring day. She caught sight of the pair and began to make her way toward them.

"I assume the two of you have a good excuse for being fifteen minutes late for class. Please go get your gear on and join the others." Deidre smiled, but Abby could tell the smile was only for Theo. She had given up trying to get Deidre to like her, settling instead for the woman's dislike. "You're going to make up those minutes in combat, to my liking."

Abby rolled her eyes and headed toward the shed where the fencing togs were kept, but secretly a wry smile perked along the side of her mouth. In her mind's eye, she was already painting targets on Theo's subtle frame.

CHAPTER 03

Salt Lake City, Utah

Brent Joby straightened his tie and cleared his throat before stepping up to the bar and motioning to the bartender. He didn't have to speak to make his order, he'd had the same thing every time he'd ordered, every day, for at least the last ten years. The clean-cut tanned man behind the counter nodded respectfully, then turned and started mixing a Long Island Iced Tea.

There was a blonde woman next to him at the bar wearing nothing but a thong, preparing a tray of jello shooters to bring around to the other patrons. She was thin and fit, but her spray-on tan was uneven and made her look blotchy and dirty. Her breasts were petite and perky and caught his attention for the better part of a minute.

She turned to him and smiled.

"How're things?" he asked, looking from her chest to her eyes and then back again. "Anyone giving you any trouble?"

"It's midday," she shrugged, making them bounce. "There's never any trouble now. Just regulars."

"Is everyone drinking?"

"A little early, isn't it?" she almost laughed, then bit her lip as the bartender slid his drink in front of him. She tensed, waiting for a stern word.

He gave none, just smiled. "It's always happy hour somewhere," he joked, toasting her before taking a drink. "Try to get them drinking though, even if it's just shooters or cola. The two drink minimum does not have a time limit."

"I'll do my best," she smiled, then finished filling her tray.

His eyes went down her backside and then back up again. "I'm sure you will. How'd you like to make a little extra on the side..."

"Cindy."

"Cindy. Just come up to my office in about five minutes."

She gave him a look.

He smiled. "I'm having a poker game tonight and my usual waitress bowed out. Thirty bucks an hour, plus tips."

Her eyebrows shot up, a smile coming to her lips as all suspicion faded away. "Sounds great."

"Great," he said, touching her shoulder blade gently as he turned away from her and walked toward the stage.

From inside the club, one would never have known it was early afternoon. There were no windows, and while the house lights existed they were never on. The lights that were on were faded and filtered into soft hues of red and blue, accompanied by a series of small lasers that were timed to the beat of whatever song was playing. The effect was similar to perpetual twilight, casting odd multiple shadows on every person and object in the room.

There was a large man sitting close to the front with precious little hair and glasses that looked like telescopes. His eyes were fixated on the dancer's every move to an extent that bordered on precognitive, having seen her routine so many times that he knew where she was about to go and what she was about to do. He clutched a gaggle of dollar bills in his stocky, rough fingers, holding them just under his chin as if it were a life preserver.

The only other two patrons in the bar were two college-aged men sitting in the back, tapping and rousing each other excitedly every time the performer made any sort of motion with the pole. They were loud and rambunctious and any other time of day Brent might have had a word with them, but at the moment he couldn't have cared less.

He took a seat in the middle of the bar, slouching as he swallowed a large mouthful of his drink and cast his eyes toward the stage.

The girl at the pole was pretty enough, but was by no means one of his star attractions. He wouldn't have any of the main lineup on until later in the night, when the place was a little more populated.

She had mocha coloured skin and jet black hair that was pulled back tight in a ponytail, a serious look on her face as she went through her routine mechanically. Makeup barely covered the acne scars that dotted her cheeks and shoulders, as well as the caesarean scar that ran across her abdomen.

He lost interest in her quickly, turning to watch Cindy

infinity

as she walked past to bring the two college boys in the back their drinks. He reached into his jacket pocket and pulled out a small, clear vile with a black cap. He unscrewed it carefully, then tapped its contents onto the glass table. A small mound of white powder sat there, changing to light blue or red depending on which light was shining his way at the time. He bent down and held one nostril shut with his finger, hovering the other over the pile for a moment before sniffing back hard.

"Woo," he said, falling back into his seat. He picked up his drink again and took a several long glugs, his adams apple bobbing and convulsing with every swallow. After a moment he put down his drink and looked back at the table to make sure there were no remnants of the powder remaining. He smiled devilishly.

The lights seemed to be moving slower now, particles of dust and smoke getting trapped in them for what seemed like minutes at a time. The music began to drone as well, slowing down and then speeding back up as if it were being played on a cassette deck that was losing power.

He downed the remainder of his drink save for the ice and forced himself to his feet. The world wobbled slightly and then righted itself, though he was fairly certain that he himself had not stumbled at all. He turned to Cindy, who was still making idle chat with the college boys, and cocked his head toward the stairs. She smiled and nodded, propping her now empty tray against her abdomen. He smiled as he walked across the floor, leaving his empty glass on the bar as he passed, then hopped up the stairs into his office.

It had been less than two minutes since he'd seen her downstairs, but he was already impatient by the time Cindy walked through the curtain that divided his office from the rest of the club. She smiled at him, so big and wide that her cheeks turned into small balls on either side of her face. She was still bare breasted, and he found himself leering at them obviously.

"Glad you could make it," he said, his tone half jovial and half annoyed.

"Sorry about that," she laughed, crossing the office in two quick strides and standing in front of the chair opposite him. He motioned for her to sit and she did, crossing her legs. "The creeper in the front finally started drinking and I had to get Lex to make him a screwdriver."

"That's alright," he beamed, chuckling a little. "These things happen."

They sat in silence for a moment, neither sure of what to say next.

Finally, Cindy spoke. "So, about the job..."

"Yes, of course. Nothing to it, really. Easier than what you're doing now. My games are open bar, so you won't have to handle any cash. You should still get lots of tips though, especially with the crowd I play with." He turned away from her and opened his desk drawer, rummaging around in it for a moment to the sound of rustling paper and cackling staples. "You can dress as you please, though I'd suggest something with class if you have it. If you don't, try and find something here that fits."

She nodded, watching him as he took another vial out

of his desk, almost identical to the one he'd used downstairs. She wondered what was happening, but tried her best not to notice or even to pay attention to what he was doing.

He popped the little black cap off the vial and let it bounce across the desk and onto the floor, then emptied its contents into the palm of the opposite hand. It made a little white pile that he immediately began to smooth out with his index finger, until it covered almost the entire surface of his palm.

Cindy shifted uncomfortably. When she looked at him again, she noticed for the first time how bloodshot his eyes were.

"Now there's just the little matter of deciding whether or not you're right for the job," he sighed, a sly grin on his face. He stood up, and she could finally see the large bulge in his pants that was pulling all of the fabric tight.

Her eyes grew wide with shock as he reached down and took his penis in his hand and began to massage it with the palm covered in cocaine.

She turned and looked back toward the door, frowning and shifting uncomfortably.

He came around the desk to be in front of her. She wouldn't look at him so he placed his finger under her chin gently and tilted it up to make her do so. The skin of her neck was silky soft. He smiled.

CHAPTER 04

Salt Lake City, Utah

Koy made an odd squeal from the other room. Chad leaned back on his chair so that he could see her.

She was standing in the center of her playroom surrounded by toys, a multicoloured blanket draped over her head. Her eyes were obscured but her nose and mouth were clearly visible, drawn up in a ridiculous grin. Her hands were raised to eye-level, fingers spread and curled into claws. She wiggled them menacingly at the empty space in front of her, then roared. "Raaar!"

She threw the blanket off quickly and ran around to the empty spot on the floor, turning around as if to look at where she had been. She slapped her palms to her cheeks in shock and opened her mouth and eyes wide. "Oh no!" she cried, then ran away to the other side of the room.

He smiled, shook his head, then let his chair fall back onto all four legs and turned back to the table. There was a house of cards there that was nearly three feet high, encompassing the entire circumference of the table and composed of two and a half decks already, with another two next to him waiting to be added.

He grabbed one without looking and unwrapped the cellophane, letting it float to the floor and join the others like it. He opened the pack and tipped it upside down, jiggling it as the cards slid out inch by inch, finally plopping into his awaiting palm.

There was a small plastic rectangle offering the rules to a few rudimentary card games, like crazy eights and crib, which he discarded along with the wrapper. He brought the neatly stacked deck to his nose and ran his thumb across the top, making them whip by. As the faces and numbers flashed by they made a quick ziiiiiiip sound that he adored. Best of all was the smell, though. That new card smell that the motion fanned his way was one of his favourites, easily in his top three along with new car and new pussy.

He laid the fresh pack beside him and flipped the first card off the top, clutching it between his thumb and forefinger. It was a joker, but he paid that no mind. All that mattered to him right now was how they stacked, and nothing stacked like a Bicycle card. They had just the right mix of paper and plastic, hold and give, whatever and what-the-fuck for making houses.

He held the card at the top and bottom, bending it back and forth until it became pliable and free, a long crease forming across the middle. Then he grabbed another card, the king of diamonds, and did the same. Sticking the tip of his tongue out through his mouth without realizing it, he lifted the cards to the top of his tower, where several cards had been laid to form a spiralling floor. He leaned them against one another then let go. They jittered a little, then steadied. He smiled.

"Tad!" Koy screamed, running into the room in her own lopsided way. "See? See?" She was holding a small group of blocks that she had attached together in no particular fashion or colour, smiling as she held it up to him. As he turned she ran past him, slamming the table with her elbow.

The house of cards shook, teetering to the left and becoming a tidal wave of cards.

"No!" he screamed, raising both his hands and wincing painfully, clenching his teeth.

They continued to lean, then bent back under the force of their own motion, bending slightly to the right before finally steadying themselves again. The only ones to fall were the two newest ones he'd just placed at the top. He stopped, regarding the miracle quizzically for a moment, then turned to Koy.

She looked at him as though she expected a scolding even though the castle hadn't fallen.

He smiled at her, gesturing toward her creation. "What you got there?"

She smiled, humming happily as she held it up him. "Is a ouse."

"Yeah?" he beamed, reaching down and picking it up. "A house is it?"

"Yea. A ouse an a grrr-aff," she nodded, taking it back and looking down at it happily.

"It's a house... and a giraffe?"

"Dap," she nodded.

He paused a moment, then bent down and gave her a kiss on the head. "Okay sweetie, sure."

infinity

She beamed.

There was a knock at the door, three soft raps that came all at once. Koy made a small gasping sound, curling her mouth up into an O and looking up at Chad. They both smiled after a moment, as a forth knock came on the door.

"Is that the super secret knock?" Chad asked, clapping his knees.

Koy hummed happily again and nodded.

"Well, who is it?"

"Mmmmmmm-Aren!" she said, jumping and waving her arms into the air when she said the name.

"Well, go answer it then!" he exclaimed, laughing.

She turned and ran out of the living room toward the door. Karen was standing by the window and smiled brightly when Koy came into view, wiggling her fingers in the wave that almost everyone used for children. Koy smiled so big that her cheeks turned red, then reached for the doorknob and started to twist it back and forth. The door wasn't really locked and she couldn't really open it either way, but they let her think she was opening it and opened it themselves at the same time. Once it was unlatched, Koy pulled it open the rest of the way. "Hello!"

"Hi Angel-Face!" Karen laughed, scooping her up under the armpits and hoisting her up into the air. The motion made her shirt go up and Karen blew raspberries into her stomach, making her squeal and laugh wildly. There was a gentleness to Karen's touch that Chad had become convinced only a woman could possess... whenever he tried to tickle her, the reaction was never quite as favourable.

He walked into the room with his book bag slung over his back, grinning stupidly at the both of them. He strolled around the corner to the fridge and grabbed himself an apple, shoving it down into the backpack's main pouch.

"Leaving already?" Karen asked, holding Koy to her shoulder now.

"Just getting ready," he half-mumbled, making sure his pack was zipped tight. "Why?"

"I brought a couple movies I thought the three of us could watch together."

Chad shot her a look.

She smiled and shrugged. "Just a thought."

He looked from her to Koy and then back again, glancing at his watch. He let out a sigh. "Did you bring chips?"

"Doritos."

"... Well, I guess a few minutes wouldn't kill me."

They both smiled.

CHAPTER 05

Port Haven, California

Abby suffered through another sculpting class, a dinner of rehydrated mashed potatoes and another night of staring at the ocean. This night, however, was different. This night the waves outside crashed, and her own waves had a gentle roll.

Theodore Flaherty was going to break her. After five months as her best friend, he was finally going to break her walls down. She should have seen it coming, the way he doted on her so. She was just too busy wallowing in her memories to really see him. He was going to break her walls down, and for once, she wouldn't mind. All that time that she hadn't been paying attention, he had crept under her skin.

She stood in her familiar position leaning against the rail, and waited.

In some ways, she wished she could have come to Port Haven sooner. If she had, maybe Jasper wouldn't have died. At the same time, if Jasper hadn't died, she never would have come to Port Haven. He had been just enough to keep her from seeing the rest of her life spiral out of control. It was just that sort of catch twenty-two that she typically found snagged in her subconscious on nights like these.

She let her mind drift back to the chilly February night that had started, and ended, everything for her.

He was in the kitchen as usual, her little kitchen wench, making her dinner. It had been pasta that night, and there was tomato paste all over his apron. He was a messy chef, but he always cleaned up afterward.

Abby could still hear his singing. He was humming Ziggy Stardust *under his breath lightly as he worked, the sizzle of ground meat frying on the pan making for background music. She was curled up on the couch in the living room with their cat, Mimi.*

Mimi had been another casualty that night, on the long list of things that had blown up in Abby's face. Not the worst of them, though.

A knock sounded at the door.

He had turned to her quizzically, raising one of his bushy eyebrows. They lived in an apartment building and hadn't buzzed anyone up, nor were they expecting anyone. Save for one old woman living upstairs, they didn't even know anyone else in the building. She had shrugged back to him, scratching behind Mimi's ear.

"Do you want me to check who it is, or should we just leave it?" she called out.

"Let me go get it, hun," Jasper smiled, looking up from his cooking. "There's no need to be making my princess get up."

He wiped his hands off and walked over to the door, peering out through the peephole for a few seconds. After a moment he turned away, confused. "There's no one there." He frowned, his brow furrowed.

There was a load bang as the gun went off, blasting a single shot through the door and through Jasper's chest. Splinters and spatters went this way and that as he fell backward, the force of that invisible chunk of metal called a bullet knocking him back faster than anything ever had.

"JASPER!" Abby screamed, diving for him and sending the cat flying. She managed to catch his head with her hand, cushioning its blow against the hardwood floor and scraping the flesh from her knuckles in the process.

A pool of blood was forming on the floor where he had fallen. His head urged up and down as he tried to speak, but could not for the amount of blood surging up in his throat.

"Baby, don't do this to me!" she sobbed, trying hard to catch her breath as she forced her hands onto the gaping hole in his chest and tried to stop the bleeding. It was all over her now, her fingers saturated in hot, sticky blood. "Don't do this to me! Hang on! Hang on, damnit!"

The door crashed open and she had a split second to come to her senses before another shot went off. She ducked toward the bathroom, feeling bullets whiz through the air by her ankles, striking the hardwood floor where she had been just a second before. Another bullet embedded itself deep into the coffee table, splitting the wood.

Then she exploded.

It was as if each cell of her body were fighting to go in different directions. The heat was unbearable, every single thing caught fire...

...and then she was whole again.

She was whole, and everything around her had exploded

into flames. Everything she loved.

She had drifted after that, homeless and half out of her mind, feeling her own body was a walking time bomb that would kill the only things she had to love.

She walked the streets, nameless and faceless, squatting wherever she could.

Then one night she heard the whispers.

"Port Haven Institute. Home for gifted youths. They take in all those crazies there."

"You're pretty crazy yourself, brother."

"Not my kind of crazy. Magic kind of crazy."

It hadn't been the first time Abby had heard talk of Port Haven, but it was the first time she had given up any pretense that she was still some normal girl. She was tired now, a street kid, and a bonafide crazy to boot. She had given up being a skeptic. She was one of them now. She was a crazy.

She panhandled for a few hours, didn't get much more than a fin and a couple dimes, but that was enough. She made her way to an internet café, sat down, and googled Port Haven.

A seniors' home was the first hit, but after a few minutes of searching, she discovered what she was looking for.

Port Haven Institute. Post Secondary Education for the Abnormally Gifted.

There was no address, no application form, and no e-mail address.

Tired, she logged into her messenger account. Instantly, a message popped up.

PORTHAVENALUMNI:
Abigail Louise Fisher?

ABBYLEE:

Is this some kind of joke

PORTHAVENALUMNI:

You've been accepted to PHI.

Do not tell anyone you are leaving, you will not bring anything with you.

You will come to the bus depot, where, at precisely 12:22, a car will arrive to pick you up.

Do not ask questions. You have eight hours, at which time if you have not arrived, we will be forced to come looking for you.

We know what you are.

Abby stared at the screen shocked, the last five words staring out at her.

We know what you are.

They knew.

There were no options left. If they would come after her anyway, she would go to them. Always better to face things head on, she reasoned... but secretly, she'd wanted to go. Needed to go, in fact. If they were out to harm her, it would be better, she thought, than the life she was living now.

She logged off, paid for her time, and left.

Within the hour she was headed toward the bus depot.

CHAPTER 06

Salt Lake City, Utah

The room was pitch black, save for one light hanging from the ceiling in its center. It shone directly on a single circular table, its green felt and hardwood rim perfectly formed and without a stain or scuff.

The rest of the room actually went on for some time, though it was impossible to tell in this light. It could have ended three feet beyond or three hundred feet, there was really no way to know.

There were five chairs surrounding the table, each of them placed equal distance apart and accompanied by its own small ring in the wood to place the players drink in and, more importantly, there was already a large pile of red, white and black chips in front of each. The room always smelled new. No matter how many weeks or months it was in use at a time, it always smelled new.

Somewhere a door opened and Brent stepped though, coming into the light. He was already holding a light brown drink packed with ice, another Long Island, as he walked around to the other side of the table. A large man dressed very similarly to Brent entered behind him but stayed out of the light, taking position next to the door with his arms crossed as five other people filtered in.

Chad walked to the chair just to the right of Brent and stood behind it, tapping its back to some unknown beat as the rest of the patrons found their way in.

An overweight man named Chris Rams with long, wispy whiskers positioned himself behind the chair on the other side of Brent. He was wearing thick black sunglasses to hide his eyes, but somehow Chad still knew that he was sizing him up. They cocked their heads at each other respectfully, then both turned their attention to the other players.

A boxy woman with long reddish hair stood beside him. Kendra Jennings wasn't wearing any makeup and dressed as though it was her goal to disguise her gender, her clothing loose and baggy. She was wearing a brown toque even though it was close to ninety degrees outside, and Chad assumed it was more for luck than for warmth.

Cindy stepped between the two and placed two drinks into their respective slots. She was wearing a French Maid outfit that looked several sizes too small for her and did very little to hide a small oval shaped bruise on her left biceps. Still, she smiled sweetly at Chad and made a motion toward her lips that he was sure was meant to pantomime 'drink'.

"Snake Bite, please," he nodded, smiling back.

She shot him a quizzical look, head tilted to one side.

"Don't feel bad, nobody knows," he chuckled. "It's one-and-a-half measures of tequila and two measures of Jack Daniels, served over cubed ice with Coke."

"Right away," she nodded, then pressed her tray to her stomach and stepped back into the darkness.

Brent raised an eyebrow at him, smirking. "That's a bold drink. Never heard of that one before."

Chad smiled. "Tastes like caramel if the tequila's good. Is it good?"

He held up his glass. "Only the best."

"You should try it on your next round. Careful though... some bars call it a Mike Tyson... 'cause it'll knock you on your ass."

"I may at that," Brent chuckled, taking a mouthful of his drink.

The last player stepped forward to his chair, just to Chad's right.

It was Victor.

Brent eyed him for a moment, then smiled. "We have a new face."

Victor smiled, nodding in response.

"Not a fan of new faces around here... you look like a cop. Not a cop, are you?"

"Ex-military," he said sharply, straightening back up when he did as if his drill sergeant just walked past. "Might explain 'the look'."

Chad tried not to glare at Victor, but failed.

Brent eyed him for a moment, then shrugged and turned his attention to the entire table. "Welcome again, gentlemen," he smiled warmly, setting down his drink and spreading his arms wide. "The game is no-limit hold 'em. Blinds will start at one and two hundred and will increase every twenty minutes or when two players have been eliminated. Blinds max out at two thousand dollars.

Any questions?"

He paused. There were no comments from the table. "Then let's begin."

Everyone pulled out their chairs and sat down, most began to fiddle with the chips in front of them almost immediately and arrange them into their own little piles.

Brent turned toward the door when he was done arranging his chips to his liking and nodded. "Sigmund?"

Sigmund stepped forward with a lazy grunt, then walked over to the other side of the table to the space set for him between Chris and Kendra.

Kendra looked at him, grinning. "Your name is Sigmund?"

He cocked an eyebrow at her, not speaking a word.

She raised her hands and shuffled her chair away from him.

Reaching into his pocket, he pulled out a new deck of cards and slid them out of the pack the same way Chad had a few hours ago.

He could smell them from across the table, the scent tantalizing his senses and making his skin tickle with gooseflesh. He ignored it, leaning in a little toward Victor. "What the fuck are you doing here?"

Victor appeared to smirk, though it was hard to tell. "Playing poker," he said simply, making a small pile of red chips right in front of him to play with. "What are you doing here?"

Chad rolled his eyes, straightening back up.

"There a problem here?" Brent asked as the dealer shuffled the cards, pointing back and forth between Chad and Victor. "You know this guy? 'Cause if you know him and he's trouble you best let me know now."

Chad frowned, turning from Brent to Victor and then back again. "Naw, I don't know him."

Brent regarded him suspiciously for a moment, then nodded to the dealer who started flipping cards face-up around the table, starting with Kendra. When he reached Chad he flipped up the jack of diamonds, then stopped and handed him the dealer button. All four players handed back the cards and he shuffled for a moment, then divvied out the cards again, this time starting with Brent and continuing until everyone had two.

Chad bent back his cards and looked at them, then set them back down. A slender arm came out of nowhere and placed a drink beside him. He smiled at Cindy, picked up two red chips and handed them to her. She smiled, nodded, then walked away again.

Victor looked at his cards suspiciously. There was a three and a seven, both of clubs. He frowned, tossing them back to the dealer. "Not an auspicious start."

Chad snickered, tossing his cards out as well.

Brent seemed to mull this over, turning from those two to his two remaining opponents. He picked up a large column of chips and tossed them in, scattering them across the table. "Might as well make it a game of poker," he smiled, winking at Kendra.

Port Haven, California

Diedre held her blade out in front of her with both hands, creating an almost perfect ninety degree angle with it and her shoulders.

The field was empty now, her fencing students having left along with the fall of night, leaving only herself and her swords alone in its center. The trees surrounding them were tall and ominous, stretching up toward the moonlight with everything they had and becoming greedy fingers.

She ignored them, focusing instead on the tip of her blade.

She took a deep breath in, then let it out. In and out. In, out.

In.

Out.

She repeated this time and again, until she wasn't even aware she was doing it anymore. Until she didn't have to think about her breath and it just happened, becoming a tiny rhythm that rested between her eyes. A joyous, tingling sensation worked its way from the top of her head all the way down to her shoulders, relaxing her musculature until she was numb all over. When this wave reached her fingertips and she couldn't feel their grip on the blade anymore, the process was complete.

There was a disjointed, disconnected tingling as she lost the feeling in her palms, both arms adjusting to the weight of the sword anew. When she moved again, the blade was a part of her. It was an extension of her body as much as her sleeping fingers were and moved as such, travelling down to almost touch the ground before turning back up the other side.

She flipped, using the momentum of the metal as it fell to carry her into it and landing again an instant later. Dust kicked up all around her and she turned, moving the weapon around her in fluid, sweeping motions.

Behind her, a twig broke.

She spun wildly, the blade becoming ridged and harsh again. Her meditation was gone now, the tingling replaced with the taunt tenseness of hardened muscles and ligaments as her eyes locked along the blade's trail and into the darkness beyond.

There was nothing there, nothing except trees and shrub and that stench of pine she swore she'd never get used to.

"Who's there?" she called finally, never once lowering the blade.

Only silence answered.

"Whoever you are, you aren't good enough to fool me," she said, her voice scolding and angry. "You'd best just come out now."

Again, silence. Somewhere an owl cooed softly at the moon, but other than that there was nothing... not even the sounds that should have been there, like the electrical buzz of Port Haven's power grid, or the security guards making their rounds.

She squinted, staring into the darkness suspiciously. "Abby?" she whispered finally, her voice surprising even herself.

There was a footfall directly behind her, along with the unmistakable sound of metal.

She spun around and raised her weapon.

Theo held an airbrush in his right hand, gently spraying a light gold shimmer onto his blades. It glided on like stardust, shimmering and shining against the sharpened metal until it looked like something not of the earth, ethereal and majestic.

He wasn't one for guns or bombs, or any other piece of crap invention that required absolutely no skill and could allow any person (especially the wrong type of people), to kill.

While he worked, he let his mind wander as only he could, touching the dreams of every sleeping person in Port Haven. He'd discovered he was a telepath not long after the Port Haven Alumni had contacted him, but it wasn't something he broadcast to the student body. The act on hearing someone else's private thoughts seemed perverse somehow... voyeuristic.

But at night he made exception to this rule, allowing his mind to touch those of his classmates. He stayed out of the more sexual of offerings (unless of course he was a feature in them, at which point he considered it fair game) and concentrated on the nightmares... there was something about a good, non-lucid nightmare that intrigued him magnificently.

A woman's scream tore through the night air and Theo's head shot up, snapping out of his trance so quickly that he thought for an instant he was still in someone else's night terror.

"Fuck!" he snapped. He ran from his studio and toward the sparring field with his katana, paint job still wet, held clenched in his fist.

As he neared the field he closed his eyes, his feet finding their way along the familiar path without his guidance.

He let his mind branch out along the walkway far faster than he could physically, discovering Deidre's presence.

Her mind was a clouded wreck, focused on another someone, someone bad. He felt her lunge at the attacker, and then nothing.

The shock of her death sent him tumbling into the blackness.

Salt Lake City, Utah

A beep came from Victor's breast pocket that made the other two remaining players turn toward him. He smiled, raising a hand in apology. "Sorry about that," he said, reaching in and pulling out a small cell phone and pressing a button on its side.

"Supposed to check your phone at the door," Brent reminded him, shooting him an annoyed look.

"Sorry," Victor said again, smiling honestly. "The little woman would have killed me. May I text her back?"

Brent paused for a moment, twiddling a chip between his fingers, then nodded.

Victor flipped the screen up to reveal a keypad, tapped several keys and then closed it again. "Thank you. I'll turn the ringer off."

Chris and Kendra had been taken out hours ago and had since left. The dealer had taken one of their chairs after Brent had noticed the sweat on his brow under the light. Cindy had taken the other but had dragged it over to the side of the room, waiting for one of the player's drinks to be empty.

There was a large stack of black chips in front of Brent, a similar pile next to Chad. Victor appeared to only have half as many, and had managed to hang onto a few reds and whites as well.

"Caught some drawl in your mouth," Brent mumbled as he got two new cards and checked them. "You up from Arizona?"

"Originally," he nodded, bringing his own cards up to his face and then lowering them again. "She's calling about Southern California, though. Apparently there's something there work's been calling me about."

"What do you do?"

"Head hunting," he answered, tossing four thousand in chips into the pot.

Chad and Brent both shot him a look.

He grinned. "Business head hunting. We try to steal sales and managers from other companies and bring them over to ours."

"Interesting move," Chad said, matching his bet. "Military to head hunting?"

"Well, I was going to stand outside the bus station and beg for change... but that job was already taken."

They all chuckled.

Brent matched the bet as well. "Call." He raised his glass to his lips again and got nothing but ice, then raised it into the light and jiggled it back and forth.

Cindy responded almost immediately, laying a fresh drink beside him. "You wanted one of Mr. Matthews' this time, right?"

"Yes," he said, winking at Chad. "We'll give that a shot."

Chad raised his glass in a mini-toast. Brent did the same.

He took a sip, swished it around his mouth, and then smiled. "That is good," he said, running his hand down Cindy's backside.

She winced uncomfortably.

Victor did the same, a slight twitch in his cheek.

Brent kept his hand there for a moment, then his eyes became dark and his face taut. He turned to the dealer and glared. "We gonna get a fucking flop, or what?"

Victor smiled.

The dealer burned a card then placed three face down on the board, flipping them all at once with one quick motion of his wrist. Seven of clubs, six of diamonds and the queen of spades.

"Where was she last time?" Victor laughed. "Two thousand."

Chad called.

Brent called. "Bitch never comes when you want her to," he said, winking at Cindy.

The dealer snapped a five of spades in line with the rest.

"Check," Victor said, quickly and quietly.

Chad tapped the table in front of him twice.

Brent looked at Victor long and hard. The man didn't look back for a long time, and when he finally did he looked away again quickly. Brent smiled, reaching into the pocket of his blazer and pulling out a small vial.

Cindy cringed.

Victor turned toward her again, narrowing his eyes.

"Anyone mind?" Brent asked, looking from Chad to

Victor and then back again.

Chad shook his head, motioning to him as if to say 'be my guest.' Victor said nothing.

"Thanks," he sighed, popping the small black cap and tapping the vial's white powdery contents onto the polished hardwood in front of him. He grabbed one of his cards, using its sharp edge to mould the coke into a little line. Pressing one nostril shut, he bent over and snorted. When he raised his head again, the drugs were gone. "Right!" he said happily, checking his cards once again. "Where were we? Eight thousand."

Victor watched as he put an entire stack of black chips into the pot, cursing under his breath. "Fold," he said, slapping his cards down in front of the dealer.

Brent smiled.

Chad leaned to one side, eyeballing one of his own black stacks. He picked it all up except for the last three, throwing them into the center. "Call."

The last card turned, the jack of hearts.

Brent remained stone faced.

Chad tapped twice on the table.

"Ten thousand," Brent coughed.

"All in," Chad said immediately, almost cutting him off.

Brent turned to him quickly in shock, frowning. He checked his cards again. Jack - ten. He looked at his chips, then at Chad's, then tossed his cards to the dealer. "Fuck."

Chad raked in his chips, then tossed his cards down face up. Six-ten.

Brent's face turned pink, but he laughed it off. "Son of

a bitch. Nothin'... you had nothin'."

Victor winced, looking from Chad to Brent and then back again. He turned and leaned over his chair, motioning Cindy toward his empty glass.

"Sorry," she said, reaching around him to take it.

"It's alright," he smiled, handing her his last few white chips. "Get me one of those Mike Tyson Snake Bite things as well... it seems to be working out pretty well for the kid there," he laughed, poking a finger toward Chad.

Chad smiled at him, possibly for the first time since they'd sat down. "It's the juice all right."

They all laughed.

When Cindy walked back around with Victor's drink, Brent looked her up and down again and smiled sinisterly. She seemed to feel his gaze on her, gooseflesh popping up along her arms and legs as she bent over and placed Victor's drink in front of him. She looked over her shoulder just in time to see him lick his lips, and shuddered.

Victor's eyes darted to hers and they met briefly. After a moment that seemed like hours, his eyes upturned in pity. "It'll be okay," he assured her, touching the back of her hand.

"Can we play poker now? Or are you two not done with your little love-in?" Brent scoffed, glaring across the table.

Victor shot him a harsh look.

Brent straightened in his seat and cleared his throat, but did not approach the matter further.

Sigmund finished handing out the cards. Victor continued to stare down Brent as he reached for his, peeling their corners back to reveal the ace of hearts and the king of spades. He smiled, lacing his fingers together and leaning his nose on them.

Chad checked his own cards briefly, then placed a stray black chip on them as if to keep them in place. "Check."

Brent looked at his cards, then quickly took a glug of his drink.

Victor squinted.

"Two thousand," he said, sliding the chips forward.

Victor looked from the chips to the man and then back again, casting one last sideways glance toward Chad. "Call."

"Call," Chad chimed, tapping the table again.

The dealer burned one card, then placed three face down again and flipped them with a flick of his wrist. One went a few inches further than intended, but nobody seemed to mind. They were the two of diamonds, the king of clubs and the king of hearts.

Victor smiled again, fighting the urge to check his cards. Trip kings, with an ace kicker. He raised his eyes to Chad expectantly.

"Check," he said, rubbing his top lip with one finger.

Brent smirked, shoving a large chunk of his chips forward. "Four thousand."

Victor let out a long breath, trying his best to appear contemplative. "Call four thousand," he sighed after a moments thought, pushing the chips forward.

"Calling," Chad said, grabbing two smaller stacks and pushing them in.

The dealer burned another card, then peeked at the turn before laying it down, smirking a little to himself. It was the ace of spades.

"Death card," Victor commented, no longer able to hide his smirk. He now had a full house.

"Maybe for you," Brent retorted, wagging a finger at him comedically.

"Check," Chad said, as if the other two hadn't spoken.

"Like a broken record, this one," Brent laughed, giving Chad a friendly tap on the shoulder. "Eight thousand."

"Classic double-up, is it?" Victor smiled.

"You read that in a book, college boy?"

"I did actually," Victor chuckled, gathering his chips and putting them in. "Can you read, you ignorant pup?"

The smile left Brent's face.

"That puts me all in," he said, tossing in his very last chip.

"Call," Chad said, still refusing to comment on the increasingly volatile banter going on between the men to either side of him.

Brent turned to Chad and nodded. "Man knows how to play poker."

The last card laid, the two of hearts.

"Check," Chad said for the final time, tapping the wooden rim of the table.

"Sixteen thou, I take it?" Victor asked, pointing at Brent.

Brent curled his lip. "Sixteen thousand."

Victor watched him, narrowing his eyes and smiling.

"All in," Chad said, pushing his chips forward. The last one he threw in was the one that had covered his cards, tossing it haphazardly into the pile.

Both men turned to him as if just now realizing he was there. Even Cindy's eyes shot up.

"That will put you all in as well," the dealer said, turning to Brent.

"I know," he barked, shoving his chips forward. "I can count."

"Just not read," Victor mumbled.

"Shut your face," he snapped again. "Wadda you got, smart mouth?"

Victor eyed him for a moment, then smiled, turning over his cards. "Full house, kings over aces."

"Whew," Brent said, letting out a little laugh and leaning back in his chair. "That's a good hand."

Victor nodded, reaching for the chips.

Brent raised a hand for him to stop, then flipped his own cards. He had pocket aces. "Full house... aces over kings."

Victor's face sank as Brent started to reel in his winnings.

"Ahem," Chad coughed, clearing his throat.

Brent turned to him, as if expecting congratulation.

He flipped over one card, the two of clubs. He flipped over the second card, the two of spades. Four deuces. Quads.

Brent's eyes went wide. "Son of a bitch."

"Son of a bitch is right," Victor laughed, leaning forward. "You have any idea how rare that is?"

"Is it?" Chad asked, bringing in his chips.

Brent looked as though he were about to speak, then stopped himself. "Good game."

"Thanks," Chad smiled, extending a hand to him.

"You too."

Victor's gaze shifted from one to the other.

Brent hesitated a moment, then took the man's hand and gave it a solid pump. "You ever consider playing professionally?"

"No."

"You should... could use some good players on my team. Tend to jot over to Atlantic City twice a month and make five mil between eight players easy... your cuts not that big, but it's still good money."

"That's okay," Chad smiled, taking a handful of chips and handing them to Cindy. "I don't think I'll be doing this much longer anyway."

"Why would you?" Victor smirked as he got up. "Couple more hands like that, you'll be set for the year."

"Hnn," Brent hummed, straightening his tie. "You can cash out at the front desk there."

Chad nodded, picking up his chips and giving a quick nod to the rest, then walked to the exit.

Victor watched him go, then turned back to Brent. "Some hand, huh?"

"Yeah."

"I mean, I got a bit cocky there toward the end... but Jesus. That put me right in my place."

"Yeah," he repeated, finally looking at him. "You need any help finding the exit?"

Victor stared at him a moment. "No." He stood up, then extended an open palm to Brent.

Brent looked at it a moment, frowned, then took it. He didn't shake it so much as he squeezed it, with enough force to cause a lesser man pain. "Good game."

"Good game," Victor smiled, taking back his hand and looking at it. There were flecks of white, powdery residue on it. His smile broadened.

"Have fun head hunting."

He nodded, then made his way toward the exit. The dealer moved to follow, as did the waitress.

"Cindy," Brent barked, stopping her dead in her tracks.

She shivered, then turned around to face him. "Yes?"

"My office, please."

CHAPTER 07

Salt Lake City, Utah

Chad stepped out of the bar and onto the street, taking one last look at the wad of cash the bartender had given him before shoving it deep into his pocket. The money was soft and warm, and he loved it. It was one of the only things manufactured by man that he preferred to have used rather than new. He liked new cards, new cars and new pussy... but he liked his money so old you could barely see the President's face.

It was long since dark out, the only light coming from the street lamps. The mountains were still visible between the buildings, but were only a jagged blue outline of moonlight across the skyline, as though someone had started to paint it and left it unfinished. The air was crisp and cool, the heat of the day wearing away as the moisture of the grasslands ebbed its way into the atmosphere and found its way over the city.

The street was a small one, less than five entrances on either side connecting two much longer streets. The sidewalk here was cobblestone, with the name of each business engraved in a piece of granite in front of each doorway like a permanent welcome mat. They were dated however, with only one still showing the correct business name. The rest were like headstones, showing the name of the now-deceased livelihood that had once prospered there. The buildings on the surrounding streets loomed high above this one like bullies, seeming to lean over above him as the light from the moon played tricks with the metal and glass, making it bend at odd angles.

He fiddled his finger across the edge of the bills in his pocket again, then forced himself to stop. Paranoid images flashed through his head of his pocket turning itself out when he removed his hand, spilling the bills to the street with a sound too soft for him to hear. He told himself that it was impossible, but still poked his head over his shoulder to make sure he hadn't dropped anything on the street behind him.

Smirking, he took out a small red cell phone and flipped the screen to the side, revealing a keypad and typed

Still on fr toNite?

He waited until the small animation of an envelope on the screen had a check mark above it, then slid it back into his pocket as he rounded the corner.

"You have any idea what the chances of that were?" Victor asked, leaning against the wall.

Chad stopped short, bringing his hands up quickly to defend himself.

Victor just stood there, staring him down. The main street wasn't empty, several cars passing by and a few drunk gents helped each other walk across the street.

They did little to make him feel more safe, and suddenly the bills in his pocket weighed a ton.

"I've got a gun," Chad said, backing up a pace.

"No you don't," Victor scoffed, pushing himself off the wall and rolling his eyes. It was odd. This was the first real emotion Chad had seen in the man, and it was pure annoyance. "People who carry guns are people scared of being attacked. People scared of being attacked are people who have been attacked in the past, and I'm willing to bet you never have been."

Chad didn't answer, shrinking into himself just a little.

"Relax. I don't need the money."

"I won it fair and square. You wanna take out your losses, go home to your husband."

His brow furrowed. "I'm also not mad at you for winning. I would've lost even if you hadn't been in the hand, anyway."

"What the hell do you want then?"

Victor paused to organize his thoughts, taking another step forward. "I simply want to know: do you have any idea what the chances of you winning that hand the way you did are?"

Chad stared at him quizzically for a moment, as still as a picture with one eyebrow raised. "No," he said finally, his posture relaxing just a little but still very on edge. "What difference does it make?"

"The odds are astronomical. At least three hundred to one if my math is right, and it always is."

"Huh."

"I used to love poker. Had a real head for it... could figure the odds right. Still lost a lot though, couldn't bluff for crap, especially when I played with family. Still, I played the percentages... you though, I think you play on luck."

"Yeah," he said, growing stern. "What of it?"

Victor smiled, wide enough that it could be seen under his facial hair. "I'm looking for people with just your sort of luck, Chad. People that can help me, help you. Help the world. Am I making any sense?"

"None," he laughed bluntly. "Sounds like you're selling religion, actually."

"Well, I'm not."

"Good. Just bought some Hindu yesterday, not gonna be buying any more for a while."

"Ha!" Victor laughed. It was a real, honest laugh right from the diaphragm. "I've heard a few in my time... never that one, though. No, what I'm trying to get together are just talented people. People who... have a knack for certain things, I guess you'd say."

"Like cards?"

"Sure. That'd be one good example."

"Well, like I told Brent... I don't see myself doing this much longer. Another two weeks, should have enough for me and Koy to live fine. For a few years, at least."

"Hmm," Victor grunted, nodding. "Well, offer's on the table... though I'd watch out."

Chad re-tensed. "Why?"

"Some people might not take this quite as easily as they seem. People like Brent Joby back there."

"Well, rough as he is, he's never stalked me all day and then snuck up on me in an alley to ask me out. So, what do you know?"

"I know he's a deviant. I know he's got a bad coke habit that he lies about and is most likely impotent without it."

The statement took Chad by surprise. "And how the hell would you know that?"

"Did the math," he drawled, all the emotion gone from his face again. Even his eyes were blank, like staring into a mannequins face. "My math's always right."

A low tone of vibration interrupted the awkward moment, and Chad reached into his pocket for his phone and flipped it open.

Yes ;) -- Suzie

appeared on the screen. He smiled. "Well, listen," he started, turning back to Victor. "Not that it hasn't been fun... I mean, it hasn't, but I've really got to be going."

"Date?"

"No."

"Girlfriend?"

"She's a friend and she's a girl. Not my girlfriend."

Victor smiled. "Hope you're packing," he said, reaching into his pocket and pulling out a small rectangular piece of paper and a pen. "I have this feeling you're going to be getting lucky tonight."

"This more of your math talking?"

"Yes, actually," he said, pressing the paper against the wall for support and scribbling something onto it. He turned back to Chad, handing it to him. "Listen, here's my contact info. I'd honestly love to stay here too, but there really is something in California that needs my attention."

"More head hunting?"

"Yes, actually. You don't need to call... but you always

can. The offers open-ended. You get yourself into any trouble, you give me a ring. No strings attached."

"No strings, huh?" he snorted, taking the card. "Funny how the people that say that are always the ones pulling them."

Victor nodded. "That's actually a pretty smart attitude. And you're not wrong, I'm not telling you everything. I do have my own interests... but they'll be put aside to serve what's best for yours the second you dial that number."

Chad eyed him for a moment, then put the card in his pocket along with the money. "I really gotta go."

"Me too," he nodded, starting off in the opposite direction as Chad. "Take care of that kid, huh? She's a sweetheart."

Chad watched him for a moment to make sure he was actually leaving, then turned and started the walk home.

Chad lay in bed with his back against the headboard, his fingers laced behind him.

Suzie lay next to him on her belly, her arm stretched across him and her bare back clean and beautiful in the light from the window, making the thin layer of sweat on her glow wonderfully. He stared at her for a moment, then turned and looked out the window.

He didn't sleep that night.

CHAPTER 08

Port Haven, California

Theo awoke blearily, the sunlight filtering onto him through the trees. The air was warm and a slight breeze blew through the leaves, sending pellets of dust against his cheeks. He could smell blood, that coppery tinge too familiar to be ignored. Retching, he rolled over onto his knees, grabbed his katana, and pushed himself up. Limping once, he dragged himself toward the sparring field.

As it came into sight, he could see a mass of people standing at its entrance. He glided over to the group slowly and melted through the crowd, moving from person to person and making his way to the front.

He already knew what he would see, the image imprinted in every single mind in the crowd.

Deidre's body lay sprawled in the dirt, limbs splayed in every direction. Her blood had congealed and dried into her hair, matting it into a mass of crimson. She looked younger than she ever had in the time he'd known her, the muscles of her face finally relaxed.

There was a long gash running from her left cheek all

the way down to her chest, splitting her right down the middle. The crowd was silent.

Professor Grayson and several other professors barred most of the scene from sight, huddled together and talking amongst themselves.

Theo could catch only bits of their discussion above the noise of the crowd.

"Not even her best student could have done this to her..."

"We can't have everyone running all over campus when there's a killer on the loose, that's not right."

Then Grayson's voice. "Tell them there will be no more classes for today then. Put in a curfew. For god's sake, someone do *something*."

The other professors looked at each other, then split off from the group and began herding the students back toward the main building.

Theo nodded and obliged when they reached him, walking back to his studio. When he was out of sight he ducked behind a bush and turned around, darting through the shrubs and jumping out next to Grayson. "Sir!"

"Sweet Jesus, Flaherty," he gasped, clutching at his chest. "What are you doing there?"

"I was there, sir. I was just over there when Deidre died," he paused, waiting to see if the other man would speak. "I was painting when I heard her cry out. I tried to come help, but passed out. I need to check if any of my weapons are missing."

"Lead the way," Grayson nodded, turning pale. "If any of your blades are missing, they could be used in an another attack. We need to make sure they're all accounted for."

The pair slipped out of the clearing quietly, making the ten minute walk to Theo's studio in complete silence. It gave Theo time to peek inside Grayson's mind for answers.

Flashes of memory assaulted him. Dimly lit rooms, a burning apartment building, a man and woman fighting.

They reached the studio and to Theo's horror the door was swinging open in the breeze.

"I closed it," he said, turning to Grayson. "I'm sure I closed it."

He raced inside and ran to the wardrobe against the far wall, thrusting it open with both hands. His weapons gleaned off the light, all lined up in a row.

Relieved, he turned to Professor Grayson and smiled. "We're fine. The killer didn't take any weapons."

"Hnn," Grayson hummed, nodding.

Theo furrowed his brow, turning away from the cabinet to face the older man. "What? What is it?"

Grayson stroked his mustache, then pointed forward at a blank space on the canvas wall.

Theo followed his gaze and his face lost all tension, going slack as he tried to comprehend what he was seeing and why.

His painting of Abby was gone.

CHAPTER 09

Port Haven, California

"So you're telling me whoever killed Deidre also took the painting you did of me?" Abby asked, as she and Theo sat on her bed. He had insisted on staying with her that night in case whoever took the painting came back for her.

"It's the only conclusion we could come to," he frowned, swirling his finger back and forth on the sheets. "Students don't have anywhere to hide anything that big, besides another studio, and we checked all of them. It's the only thing that's gone."

"But why that one?" she huffed, scratching her head. "I mean, not that it isn't *good*, but--"

"I know what you mean. And I'm not sure it's what they went there to get... but once they saw it, I suppose something about it --"

Something dropped on the floor above them, hard enough to shake the ceiling and send bits of tile sprinkling down onto the sheets. Both of their eyes shot skyward, as if expecting the ceiling itself to give them some clue as to what had happened.

The crash was followed by a long, drawn out rolling sound, as though someone had spun a hubcap on the floor. Finally, there were footsteps. Short, baited footsteps that were loud one moment and soft the next.

"Shouldn't everyone be in their rooms by now?" Abby whispered.

Theo nodded, standing up from the bed slowly, never taking his eyes off the ceiling. "There aren't any other rooms above yours, are there?"

She paused a moment, then shook her head. "Why would people be up there now?"

"Not people. Person," he corrected, even as the footsteps changed to heavy once more. "It's just one person... I think it's someone breaking in."

Abby bit her lip.

"It's got to be the person that killed Deidre," he decided, heading toward her bedroom door purposefully. "I'm not going to let him get away again."

"You can't possibly think you can take him," she spat harshly, grabbing him by the arm and spinning him back around. "He killed Deidre. Easily. He'll kill you even easier."

"If you're so afraid I'm gonna get my ass handed to me, why don't you come along and help?" he smirked, shrugging out of her grasp. "Two against one should be an easy match. Besides, we'll catch him by surprise."

"You're *not* serious."

"Coming?" he asked impatiently, though with a mischievous grin on his face. He picked up his katana and darted out of the room into the darkness.

Abby rolled her eyes, huffed, then followed.

CHAPTER 10

Port Haven, California

They crept up the stairs of the West Tower, the sound of a struggle growing closer every second.

There were four towers within the grounds of Port Haven. Each was a mirror image of the other, stretching up three stories (although steep and winding staircases made it seem much taller). When the school had been built there had only been the ground level and the towers, giving a castle-like air, but as more floors were added the towers were reduced to the function of stairwells, connecting the original structure to the additional floors.

Forty years ago the towers had been wired for electricity to eliminate the need for oil based lighting, but those old lamps were still perched between the mortars and now seemed to ebb out darkness from their burnt wicks, fighting the buzzing invasion of fluorescence every chance they got.

Abby stared at the lanes and grooves in the brick as she walked up behind Theo, the faces her imagination made in them peering out scornfully at her. She shivered, turning her attention up to the top of the stairs.

The door to the third floor was wide open, grunts and gasps escaping from it more and more with every second.

Theo turned back at squinted at her, as if judging her readiness somehow. "It'll be okay," he assured her, turning back toward the action but laying a comforting hand on her shoulder as he did.

"I know," she said, sneering a little and rolling her eyes.

He opened his mouth to respond, then didn't as the hallway beyond the door finally came into view.

Professor Grayson fell to the floor in a shuddering mound of fat, his rotund midsection providing him some cushioning, but not much. He looked to twitch briefly, but did not move otherwise.

The attacker was nowhere in sight, just a long, brightly lit hallway filled with dorms and lecture halls like any other.

"Professor!" Abby hissed in shock, stepping past Theo to go to him.

Theo reached out and grabbed her arm. "He's fine."

"How do you know?"

He paused. "Just do."

Abby tisked, shrugged out of his grip and ran the rest of the way up the stairs to Professor Grayson, shaking him.

Theo huffed and ran behind her, just reaching the door when it slammed shut.

Abby heard the sickening click of the door locking, followed immediately by Theo's fists as he began to bang on the door furiously.

"Hello Abby, darling," a soft male voice cooed. "If you could drop your sword, that'd be nice. I'd really rather not have to fight you off. I don't want to accidentally hurt you."

All the colour drained from her face and she bit her lip. Her gaze shifted slowly from Grayson (who was breathing, albeit weakly) to the sword that was still clasped tightly in her hand. She looked at it as though it would somehow tell her what to do, whether or not to listen to whomever it was behind her... and on some level she was aware that if this person had indeed bested both Deidre and Grayson, it mattered very little.

In the reflection of the flat of the blade she could see him, still standing by the door with one hand rested on it. He was wearing all black clothes that seemed to fit tightly to his slim form, his skin an almost iridescent pale hue that the moonlight glinted off as gently as it glinted off his own swords. Two of them, in fact.

She squinted, tilting her head slightly as she stared at him.

She gasped and her heart dropped as she turned to face him, his fingers coming loose on the blade's handle.

Black shaggy hair covered most of his face, but glinting through his long bangs were golden eyes, exactly the same as Jasper's. He was even the same height, and looked about the right age.

If it wasn't Jasper, it was his twin.

"Come on, Abby," he laughed, and it was Jasper's laugh... though not quite. "We both know you're no match for me."

"How are you here?" she whispered, squinting suspiciously.

"Darling, I'm here the same way everyone else is. Well, almost the same way. You all come in through the door, I happened to come in through a fifth story window."

"That's not what I mean! I saw you die," she sobbed, collapsing to her knees as her grip on her sword loosened even more. "How are you back here?"

"I don't know who you think I am, but I never died, darling. In fact I am very much alive right now, and always have been since the day I was born." He had a look on his face that was a cross between worry and a smirk. He transferred both swords to one hand and offered the other to her openly. "Now, shall I help you up so we can talk?"

Abby's head snapped up, as if something in her kicked her back to reality upon seeing his hand. "Who are you?"

"Someone who wants to help you choose the right path." He winked at her. "I don't want to have to choose it for you."

Abby went cold at his words. "Is that what you did for Deidre? Is that what you've done for Grayson? Don't think I'm going to let you do the same to me."

Gripping her sword handle so swiftly that she felt the leather straps twist, she brought her blade forward toward the stranger's chest. It was like kismet when it happened, nothing by intention and everything fate. Deidre had taught her to move like liquid... to flow as naturally as though the sword were an extension of her body. And it was true that often, after hours of practice with the blade, instead of feeling tired she would feel a sort of phantom pain after setting it down. As though she were missing that section of herself.

Nobody had been able to match her in swiftness, not even Deidre.

In the blink of an eye, he had a sword in each hand with her sword caught between his blades.

Her breath caught in her throat as she tried to free herself. Her face was only inches from his now, exhaling together after a tense moment, the air colliding between them and making a small cloud of mist.

"What do you want from me?" she managed to say, too shocked to say anything that sounded intelligent.

He smiled. "I need you to come with me. Me and Victor. It's for your own protection. Otherwise you'll just have them after you again."

She stopped struggling to free her sword, a confused look crossing her face.

The man let go of his own blades, sending her stumbling backward.

She caught a frightened look in his eye, and realized with horror that she was falling toward the window.

The man raced forward, slipping his arms under her just in time, then twirling around so they were in the center of the room. Their eyes locked.

Jasper raced forward, slipping his arms under her just in time, then twirling around so they were in the center of the room. Their eyes locked, and Abby let out a twinkling burst of laughter. "You always save me just in time."

Surrounding them was what was left of their dinner. Diced carrots, rice and potatoes covered the rug. Mimi had slunk behind the couch, hissing.

"Damn cat, always getting underfoot," Jasper joked. "Seriously though, you've got to be more careful. I don't want to think about what would happen to you two if I wasn't here."

"Abigail! Are you listening? I have to go now!" the man barked, grabbing her cheeks and snapping her back to reality. "Theo's going to open the door any moment, but I need you to be ready when I come back. I promise you I'm going to convince you. Next time you have to come with me."

His eyes were like fire. He laid her to the ground, placed her in a sitting position, and picked up his swords. With a final look over his shoulder, he leapt toward the window and out into the night.

The door burst open, Theo stumbling in head first.

She saw that his eyes seemed guarded, as if he knew what had just went on in her mind. She dismissed the notion almost immediately. No matter how thick or thin the door was, there could be no way Theo could see into her thoughts.

"You're okay, right?" he asked, already on his way to check on Grayson.

She mumbled something that sounded like an affirmative, though Theo took no notice. She hated that he looked worried, but hated more that he obviously knew more than he was letting on.

She got up slowly and strode over to the window.

There was nothing there.

"I'm going to get the nurse, okay?" she sighed, turning back to where Theo knelt with Grayson. "Meet me back in my room after, if you can."

CHAPTER 11

Salt Lake City, Utah

"Call," Brent said, pushing a small stack of chips forward. He smirked devilishly to himself, taking a long drink from his glass. It was a snake bite again today, and he raised it to Chad from across the table before he drank.

Chad did the same, checking his cards with one hand as he raised his own glass to his lips with the other.

To Brent's left was a man in his early forties wearing thin glasses and a plain navy-blue tee shirt. He was balding except for the back, which had been trimmed down to scruff, and his arms were covered in tattoos. They weren't quite sleeves, but close. There were leopards, portraits of his children, a memorial cross for his mother, a skull, a fuzzy looking die and a few that were simply dots. Some were coloured, others were done in an odd blueish hue and were so blurry they were almost unrecognizable. He had an infectious, childlike grin and mischievous eyes, but large upper arms that led one to believe that he was better at giving humour than receiving it. He stared at the pile of chips seriously, but there was always a snicker waiting just beyond his lips.

Brent watched him, tapping two fingers back and forth on his glass. "We ain't got all day, Ed."

The man shot him a look, then let out a little laugh. It was a condescending little chuckle, as though he felt he'd just been given lip by a child. "I'll call."

Chad reached for the pile of chips he'd had prepared while waiting for Ed and threw them forward, scattering them across the center of the table. "Call."

The man to Chad's right let out a long sigh, shuffling in his seat as the dealer burned one card and discarded it and then flipped the turn card. It was a three of hearts, just a little tattered on one edge. It joined the king of hearts, two of diamonds and five of clubs, sliding in just to their right.

"Well that's a mess," Steve laughed, tapping the ash from his cigarette. Cindy leaned over in front of him, replacing his empty drink. He smiled at her, sliding her one of his chips. "I think I'll check this one."

Brent fiddled with his upper lip a moment, then grabbed a large stack of chips and pushed them in. "Two thousand."

"Pshh-ew," Ed sighed, again laughing a little. "That's a bet."

"Too rich?"

"No... no, not too rich. Just... that's a bet, is all," he said, trying to qualify his statement. He reached down and grabbed the chips, pushing them forward. He had less than a thousand left.

"Call and put you all in," Chad frowned, glancing

at Ed's remaining chips and then putting in his own to match. "One thousand three hundred more."

"Thirty-three hundred to you," the dealer repeated, motioning to Steve.

"I know," he replied, mildly annoyed. He looked at his cards once more, then tossed them away. "Bullshit."

Brent grabbed the remaining thirteen hundred, pushing them into the middle without a word.

Ed did the same, sliding all his chips forward before leaning over and giving Chad a friendly tap on the arm. "Gunning for me this time?"

Chad smirked. "Not really."

"Oh, I know," he chuckled. "Just a game."

"Can we play it, then?" Brent huffed, waving impatiently to the dealer.

The dealer shot him a look, then flipped the river. It was the two of hearts.

Ed laughed.

Brent scoffed. "All in," he droned, pushing all his chips forward.

Ed laughed again.

Chad watched it for a moment, as if waiting for the chips to do something. He pushed his own forward save for two hundred, matching Brent's stack for stack. "Call."

"Well I think somebody knew something I didn't," Ed laughed, flipping his two cards. They were the five of hearts and the three of diamonds. He was already standing up from his chair as they hit the table. "I doubt that's the winning hand."

"You'd be right," Brent smirked, turning over a two of

clubs... and a king a diamonds. "Two pair, kings high."

Ed chuckled, then gave a friendly salute to the three men before stepping away from the table.

Brent stared across the table at Chad again, his hands laced in front of him. They locked eyes for a long moment. Finally, Brent cursed. "Fucker. You got this again, don't you?"

Chad smiled, turning over his cards. Ace of hearts, queen of hearts. A flush.

Brent cursed, stepping up from the table and walking to the wall to watch the rest of the game. He glared at Cindy, still sitting on the other side of the table.

A shiver ran down her spine as the dealer started to hand out cards to Chad and Steve.

Chad collected his winnings from the bartender again, counting them along with the burly man as he scooped bill after bill from his lockbox. He'd learned to count quickly the last few months. Could do the math.

The bartender gave him a wary look as he handed him the final amount: six thousand dollars. Both men nodded, and Chad turned toward the exit.

"Hold up a second," Brent said, coming down the stairs behind him.

Chad stopped, turning back and smiling.

"That was some game in there tonight," Brent said, a broad smile on his lips.

"Thanks," Chad said, keeping his hand over his now bulging pocket. "You too."

"No, I mean that was amazing. You got a real talent

for the game, kid."

"... thanks?"

Brent leaned against the bar, motioning for the man behind the counter to get him another drink. "You given any more thought to my offer? Come work for me, play for me?"

"Like I said, not looking to go pro," he nodded, averting his eyes. There were white marks under Brent's nose he was trying very hard not to look at. "I'm doing pretty good on my own."

"Yeah, you are," Brent nodded, clicking his tongue against the roof of his mouth. "I'd consider it though... really."

Chad shifted. There was a connotation to his voice he didn't much like. "I don't think I'm going to be playing much longer either way."

Brent nodded. "Perhaps you should find somewhere else to play. Some people... some people might not like getting beat quite that often." His voice was cold and hateful.

Chad shifted uncomfortably again. "But not you."

"Me? Lord no. Wouldn't host the game if I was in it for the money. But guys like that Ed? You never know what they might do, you take enough of their money."

"Yeah..." Chad said, nodding quickly and trying desperately not to look nervous. "Yeah. Think it might be a good time to switch houses."

"Or retire."

"Or that... yeah."

"Okay," Brent laughed, clapping Chad on the back heartily. "But you ever want to come work for me, you let me know okay? We can always use players like you... people that know the game. You can always knock on my door, you understand? Anything goes wrong... you come back here." He gripped Chad's shoulder now, just a little too tightly.

"Yeah," Chad replied, stepping away. "I'll do that."

"Good stuff. You have a good night, friend."

Chad turned and walked down the staircase, exiting the building to the alley outside.

As soon as the door closed behind him, he threw up.

CHAPTER 12

Port Haven, California

Abby awoke to rays of sunlight sliding across her face, with the type of sudden alertness that only comes after many hours of undisturbed sleep.

Theo was next to her, his arm having ended up draped around her at some point in the night.

She hugged his arm close to her, smelling his cologne, a hint of sweat, and the last few remnants of the sterile smell of hospital, and sighed when she realized that meant that Theo had gone down to the hospital wing.

Wondering briefly if Grayson had awoken long enough to tell him his side of the story, she shirked his arm off and slid out of bed silently. Making her way over to a clean pile of clothes, she selected a new outfit and changed.

Glancing over her shoulder at Theo to make sure he was still asleep, she opened the door soundlessly and left.

∞

The breakfast area was almost empty, save for two

teachers huddled together in deep conversation. One was a large brutish woman named Miss Fitzpatrick who had red hair and a wheat allergy that she constantly reminded anyone she was eating with of. The other was a twenty-something history professor named Mr. Graham who looked like Woody Allen's neurotic brother, with crumbs of waffles sticking to the sides of his mouth.

They turned and looked at her almost at once, their eyes filled with a glaring mistrust that she would not have expected here.

Rolling her eyes, she turned to leave again. "Sorry I came," she mumbled.

"Abigail," Mr. Graham called out, wiping the lower half of his face with a napkin as he stood.

Abby stopped, huffed once, then turned around and forced a smile. "Yes, Mr. Graham?"

"If you could kindly note, our curfew is still in place," he said, his stutter making him stumble on each K sound. "No more roaming the halls at night, understand?"

She nodded twice, in an exaggerated and sarcastic motion. "Yes. This is morning."

He shot her a horrid look. "The fact of the matter is, you were reckless trying to save Grayson. You endangered your own life and Theo's for no reason. He may stick up for you, but it's easy to see what really happened. Don't let it happen again."

Taking a deep breath, she nodded in the same manner and turned away without a word, yanking the door to the mess hall open so hard that it slammed into the far wall with a loud thud.

When it spun back around and closed, she brought

her hands up and laced them through her hair, digging her nails into her scalp. "Argh!" she growled, waking several students in the adjoining rooms, then marched her way to the nearest exit and left, stepping out into the seldom used pathways that surrounded the East Dorm.

Trees and bushes created a tangled mess that she had to force her way through. She took several deep breaths, feeling the air fill her more and more with each until she could think again.

"Fuckers," she said, turning back toward the red exit as if the door itself had committed some wrong against her. "Fuckers. This place is nuts. It's nuts and everything is nuts and I'm--"

She stopped, turning back to the foliage that surrounded her. There was a small squirrel sitting on a log about fifteen feet in front of her, its large black eyes staring at her blankly.

"Talking to myself. Yessir, I'm talking to... myself. Awesome."

She laughed, ran her hands through her hair again, then started her way down the trail, noisily making her way toward her pottery studio.

The brush here was thick and overgrown, having been left by the groundsmen for the last few seasons after the conservatory burned down. It had been the only thing at this end of the dorm, and it seemed a waste to keep all this up until it was rebuilt.

Even so, the few times she'd been there, she'd found she'd actually enjoyed it a little more than the other, better kept areas of campus.

There was an owl sleeping in a nearby tree with its

wing covering its face, suspended there by some bizarre and beautiful display of muscle memory. It looked like something out of a Disney cartoon about spring. Fade in on the sleeping owl, colourful leaves blow by playfully... cue the sparrows and: ACTION!

BANG!

A shot rang out, followed quickly by a muffled

THFFT!

that left a bullet embedded in the tree next to her. Splinters of wood sprayed in all directions as more shots came, showering down on Abby as the tiny daggers poked and prodded at her. The owl took flight almost immediately, its talons scraping briefly against the arch of her ponytail before taking off into the morning sky.

She twirled to see where the shots were coming from, barring her teeth and clenching her fists.

She caught a quick glimpse of a large tanned man not far off the trail, his face mostly obscured by the gun he had raised at her. Another shot was fired, whizzing through the air above her. She yelped and stepped backward, tripping and falling onto the gravel path in a puff of dirt and dust. She cursed herself, then tried to crawl away, but her foot was stuck beneath a root. She cursed again, then heard the swish of a sword through the air.

She breathed a sigh of relief, her first thought being of Theo.

Turning around, she was surprised to see the man from the night before standing between her and her attacker.

There was a soft plinking sound as the top of her attacker's gun hit the ground.

It was followed closely by a soft, wet sound as his finger joined it.

The tanned man's mouth was hanging open as he stared at the stump. His eyes flashed up to Abby's man in black.

"Try me," her rescuer whispered, twirling his swords and advancing. His thin figure looked fragile compared to the attacker's beefy, tattooed arms.

Abby's mouth hung open. Tattooed arms. Her eyes scanned up his right forearm and found it.

"Miss, you've never seen this tattoo before? Not on any of your fiancé's friends?" The policeman seemed kind, but Abby didn't want to look at any more pictures. None of them were helping. This one showed a tattoo of a king of aces encircled by bullets. The flesh around it was mostly burnt, but she could tell other tattoos surrounded it. *"I've never seen it. How's this supposed to help anyway?" Abby said calmly, though she felt like screaming.*

The policeman sighed. "It's the only part of him that's not too charred for identification. We're working on the dental, but it's going to be a while before we get anything back from the lab. Every ounce of time we can save in tracking down his identity can help with this case. You're lucky the fire started where it did, or you'd be dead too."

"That didn't do much for either of them, did it?"

She went off the grid hours after that. There was nothing left worth sticking around for. Police couldn't help her. Doctors couldn't bring people back. She couldn't keep the people she loved safe. Her job at Shane Industries wasn't worth going back to. No matter how great the opportunity was working as a lab assistant there, it didn't matter if she had no one to share it with.

It was better if she just disappeared.

Her attacker took off running, clutching his bleeding stump as he went.

Her savior turned briefly and smiled at her. "You better get out of here, Abby. There are more of them lurking about. I'll be back soon."

Abby raised her hand to stop him, but he turned into the foliage and disappeared as quickly as he'd arrived after the tattooed man.

CHAPTER 13

Port Haven, California

Abby found her way to class in a daze. By the time lunch came around, she still hadn't seen Theo, or told anyone what had happened. Her heart was thumping so fast she couldn't even feel the long gashes in her legs, or the deeper gash in her knee. In fact, she didn't even notice them until Theo pulled her out of the lunch line looking white-faced with terror.

"What the hell happened to you?" he hissed, searching her eyes for some sign of life.

She jumped as she was shaken out of her reverie. "I was on my way to class and some guy came after me. Ja... the guy from last night came and fought him off... He saved me, Theo."

Theo held her by the shoulders, still looking frightened. Looking even more frightened now than he had just a moment ago, she noticed.

"What is it?" she asked finally, squinting at him as she finally stood straight again. "What are you hiding?"

"The guy from last night is not Jasper, Abby," Theo

said, his voice going dangerously quiet. "That's one thought you have to shake out now. He may be a lot of things, but he is not the man you were engaged to."

"How do you…" Abby trailed off, eyes growing wide. She glared at him, shaking out of his grip. "How much do you know that you're not telling me? And don't you dare lie."

Closing his eyes he let out a deep, mournful sigh. "A lot. And I'm not going to tell you what I know. It wouldn't be right."

He bowed his head and kept his eyes closed, knowing exactly what was going through her mind.

He let her have the satisfaction of slapping him, before she turned her back and walked away from him.

She decided to go for a run instead of dinner to clear her head. It was reckless, in a way that seemed habit forming. Run headlong into a room with an armed guy who has killed one teacher and incapacitated another?

Check.

Crash through the woods by yourself when you've just been told there are people after you?

Check.

Go for a run at night, when you've been attacked that very morning?

Check.

She smiled grimly as she went over the list in her mind. Jasper had called her something once, years ago, when they'd first started dating. They'd been at an amusement park and gotten cotton candy and she'd ridden a rickety old roller coaster that had been assembled inside of thirty minutes over twenty times to Jasper's one, each time swearing the bolts in the track became looser and looser.

"What was it, lover?" she whispered to herself as she hopped over an old birch log and continued jogging. "What was it you called me?"

An adrenaline junkie. That was it. That little thing inside her that overpowered fear, doubt and, often, common sense in favor of a thrill. For as harrowing as that morning had been, it had been thrilling. She had never been that close to death... that close to *him*.

She wasn't about to forget a weapon this time though. She had a 9 mm strapped to one thigh and a dagger strapped onto the other. And somewhere, buried deep down inside... part of her knew she was looking for a fight.

Taking off along the trail that led to the beach, she ignored the rumblings of her stomach and decided to wait until after Theo had eaten to get something.

Her run was calming. Rather than the anticipated run-in with another villain, she simply jogged along the beach and circled back toward the dorms. In that odd, roller coaster way, she was almost let down.

Stopping to catch her breath along the shoreline, she bent over and leaned on her knees, looking out into the forest with her sweat-covered face.

"Are you out there, love?" she asked, scanning the tree line for any sign of movement. "Are you watching?"

She stopped herself.

As much as she hated to admit it, Theo was right. She couldn't keep thinking of this man as Jasper.

Still... the likeness was incredible.

When she finally found herself back in the common room, Abby was relieved to see that it was devoid of people. Some food was still left out, though none of her favorites. She looked down at her stomach as it gave a little rumble.

"Shut up, stomach monster." She smiled to herself. "You'll get your fill soon enough."

She heaped a pile of mystery meat and mashed potatoes onto a plate, then poured lukewarm gravy over it.

Her stomach growled in defiance again.

"It's better than nothing," she scolded, still smiling as she turned and walked back to her room.

The halls were bare as well, more so than she'd ever seen them at this hour of the day. Remembering the curfew she'd been scolded for that morning, she quickened her pace before someone saw her. Juggling her plate and a cup of cola, she opened her bedroom door.

Gasping, she dropped her dinner to the floor. The plate shattered and potatoes splashed outward in a wet lump with such force that the gravy spattered up onto the wall next to her.

The Jasper look-alike was standing in the middle of her room.

"Miss me?" he said before he walked over. He shut the door behind her and took the cola, laying it on the nightstand.

She stood frozen in place, taken off guard by the sight of him in plain clothes. Now, more than ever, he reminded her of Jasper.

"What are you doing here now?" Abby whispered.

Theo could hear everything they were saying.

He didn't bother trying to block it out, in fact. He knew he had deserved the slap in the face, deserved Abby avoiding him... but she didn't deserve him giving up on her.

For psychics, listening in on private conversations was something generally considered immoral, but this time he rationalized that it would be more immoral not to.

He didn't want it to be his fault if she did something reckless.

"You know what I'm doing here," the Jasper look-alike said, his hands so close to her arms that she could feel her short hairs dance on end with his every motion. "Now, are you going to come with me easily, or do you need more convincing?"

"Not convincing so much as explaining," she snorted. "I don't even know who you are, how you could help me. You could just want to hurt me the same as those other guys."

"Hunter Mason, at your service," he smiled, circling around and extending his right hand toward her.

"That's it, a name? That's all I get and I'm supposed to trust you?"

He smiled at her with those golden flecked eyes, his grin wild and contagious.

She placed her hand in his. It was small and dark against his perfect porcelain skin. Letting out a deep breath, she let him pull her in.

He held her in his arms, gently caressing her hair with one hand while cupping her face with the other. Beads of sweat clung to their bodies, glistening as city lights filtered in through the blinds. The sound of traffic drifted up from the street, but they heard nothing. She only had eyes for him.

Her fingers made their way to the back of his scalp, knotting in his wavy hair. Their lips met briefly, then parted. She couldn't pull her gaze away from his eyes. She had never seen anything so golden, perfect. She could have stayed there forever.

She felt his arm slip around her back, supporting her and directing her away from the door. She pulled him in, afraid to let go. Their lips met.

She felt his palm against her hip, warm and firm. He leaned down, placing a kiss on the curve of her abdomen. She felt her body flutter at his touch, and the baby kicked.

"You're not him," she forced herself to say, biting her lip and almost hating herself for saying it. "I can't keep pretending that you are. I'll go with you to Victor, but don't let me pretend you're him. It won't be fair."

Hunter paused, his golden eyes only inches from her jade ones. "Who said anything about fair?"

Abby felt her eyes lock with his, letting the trueness of his words hit her. She let her lips touch his again.

Theo blocked them out finally, not wanting to know anymore of what they were both thinking, no longer wanting to intrude on Abby's memories.

He laid back onto his bed, and cried.

CHAPTER 14

Salt Lake City, Utah

Chad skipped the steps to his patio two at a time, an odd smile on his face.

He was just getting back from Janelle's, where he'd again been visiting Suzie. He was a little later than he'd told Karen he was going to be, but he didn't think she'd mind. She never had before.

He reached deep into his pants pocket and pulled out a ring of keys, letting them jingle aimlessly against the surfboard key chain that Koy had given him a few months ago. He had no idea where she had gotten it or why, but when Karen returned with her from the market one day she had had it and claimed that it was for him. He didn't know why a surfboard reminded her of him, but it did and it melted his heart to know that she thought about him so much.

There was a plastic bag in his left hand that had a snack in it for Koy, even though she was probably in bed by now. It would be reheated as tomorrow's lunch, he decided. He slipped the bag onto his wrist to free up his fingertips, then selected the proper key and bent it down to put it in the lock.

The door pushed open easily the second the key was pressed to it, swinging slowly open until one of Koy's boots stopped it.

He felt a lump rise up in his throat as he rose slowly back to standing position, staring into his kitchen. Nothing was out of place, but it still seemed wrong somehow. It was too quiet. Koy would be asleep and Karen never made much noise, but this silence was different. This silence was deafening.

He knew right away.

"Karen?" he called out frantically, stepping through the porch and into the kitchen without taking off his shoes. It seemed dark, although he couldn't figure out why until he turned and saw that the lamp in the corner had been knocked over, sending shards of polarized glass everywhere. "Oh my God."

He ran through the hall, crinkling the bulb under his shoes. He didn't stop to notice the toys that had been knocked off their shelf in the hallway or the birthday presents that had been wrapped and stacked so neatly in the corner now tossed about. He rounded the corner and started up the stairs as fast as he could, his heart wailing in his chest. He felt his body prepare itself to cry, even though he hadn't made any tears yet. Part of him knew, and that part was bearing down.

There was a large chunk of wall missing from the side of the stairwell, followed by three long trails where the paint had been ripped away by something sharp. A knife he guessed, though he didn't stop to examine it.

He ran to Koy's room and shoved open the door.

The room was dark. The light from the doorway showed her bed, the blankets tossed back and the pillows pushed aside. It was empty.

"Koy?" he called, turning on the light and running for the closet. He knew he wouldn't find her, but whatever part of him clung to hope would not allow it to check in until it was proven.

"Koy!" he screamed, again and again, as he checked under the bed, behind the dresser, in his bedroom and even in the bathroom before heading back and checking the bed again, pulling the covers back completely to make sure she wasn't hiding in them. "Koy this is not funny! Come out here *right now!*" he yelled, his voice both desperate and angry.

He saw something on the floor that had been on the bed until a moment ago, then reached down to pick it up. It was an assortment of lego blocks snapped together in a way that would not have meant anything to anyone else, but he knew that it was both a house and a giraffe.

He knelt down on his sister's bedroom floor and started to cry.

Northton, Idaho

He gripped it between his fingers, feeling the wet snap of its bones reverberate through his hands as he broke its neck. He let out a deep breath, feeling a slight release as the creature within his grasp went limp.

He smiled, showing off those chalky, dark teeth.

He laid it down on his workbench in front of him. It

was dank and mouldy and appeared to be made from driftwood, covered with small nooks with spikes and wire and places to hold his tools. He looked around frantically, those white eyes with pink rims, like a rabbits, mulling over his inventory. There was a chipped black handle sticking out at him, wedged between his desk and the wall. He grabbed it and pulled it out.

It was covered in blood of varying colours and age, some fresh and red and others a dark old brown. It had a long serrated edge and was almost a foot in length. He brought it down hard on the creature's midsection, spattering blood back onto his slender face. He moved to wipe it off, but only succeeded in smearing it in long lines over his smooth, pale head.

He pulled it apart, the creature's skin stretching and becoming transparent as it tried desperately to remain whole, snapping away in one final burst of blood and petulance.

He chuckled softly to himself, then brought the blade back up and started to peel the rest of the skin away.

Los Angeles, California

Victor sat uncomfortably on his barstool, the cushion swaying back and forth dangerously on its slender perch. He groaned, looking down at it several times to make sure it was securely fastened before leaning forward onto the bar to try and get some of his weight off of it.

The place was small and cramped, located in a sub-basement on the east side and called itself 'The Brew'. Most of the patrons looked as though they hadn't bathed in days, and if there were any doubts the odour in the room confirmed it.

There was a mean looking Puerto Rican man by the door with his arms crossed staring right at him, looking away only to give the once over to any new patrons that came in.

An old man stood behind the bar. He looked as though he'd stepped out of a Spaghetti Western, plump and kind looking with a full and bushy gray mustache. He was cleaning the counter in the seconds between orders, and looked to be having as much fun serving drinks as his patrons were drinking them.

Victor tipped his glass back and took a large mouthful, looking for the world like a Viking with his matted blonde hair and scruff covered chin. When the glass was empty he raised it, swaying it back and forth in the bartender's direction.

"More of the same?" the older man asked, taking the glass out of his hand.

"Please," he responded, running his fingers through his hair from front to back, then scratching a particularly nasty itch at the base of his skull. The new drink was placed in front of him and he brought it back to his lips briefly before stopping. Slowly, he lowered the glass back to the table. He wiped his mouth clean of the frothy liquid, stroking his beard. "You're late."

"Cut me a little slack?" Hunter whined, stepping up beside him and leaning against the bar. "Have you ever tried to drive into the city at this hour of the day? We made it here in one piece, that's saying something."

Victor shot him a look from the corner of his eye.

"How's the beer?"

"Warm," he hissed, smacking his lips after another sip before spinning the wobbly stool to face Hunter.

He could see Abby now out of his peripheral vision, several feet away against the wall. She was looking from side to side at the bar flies that surrounded her, shuffling back and forth from foot to foot and trying not to get too close to either of them. She wrinkled her nose in disgust.

Victor frowned.

"What's the matter?" Hunter asked, cocking one of his thinly preened eyebrows Victor's way.

"I was hoping for someone with a tad more experience."

"Anyone with more experience has learned how to stay the fuck off our radar," Hunter said, motioning to the bartender. A second later he had a small glass of clear liquid in front of him that smelled like disinfectant and he immediately took a long swallow. "We're just lucky places like Port Haven are out there. If it wasn't for your contact we might not even have known about that."

Victor sighed, taking one last gulp of his drink before getting up and crossing the short distance between he and Abby. When they were so close she could feel his breath on her breasts he spoke again. His voice was soft, yet authoritative. "Abby Fisher?"

She stiffened a little, then nodded.

"You sure?" he smirked. "You don't seem so sure."

"Well I am."

He smiled at her warmly.

She relaxed visibly, her hands falling to her sides.

"You know why you're here Abby?" he asked.

She glanced over his shoulder at Hunter, who threw her a wink. "Hunter seems to think it isn't safe for me at Port Haven anymore."

"It's not safe for us anywhere," Victor warned. "Not out in the open, anyway. Not like that... tell me, Abby, do you have any idea what it is you do?"

"Do?"

It was like each cell of her body went in different directions. The heat was unbearable, every single thing caught fire, and then she was whole again. She was whole, and everything around her had exploded into flames, including everything she loved.

"No," she said defensively, breaking eye contact with Victor. "No, I don't."

He smiled. "That's okay. That's what I'm going to show you. When we're done... the world will be a better place. Infinitely better, if I may say so myself."

Hunter rolled his eyes. "Can we stop with the grasshopper routine and just get the hell out of dodge? I caused quite a stir down at the school."

Victor shot him a look, then turned back to Abby. "Sorry. Good help is hard to find."

She laughed. Hunter did too, albeit a little less honestly.

"Now," Victor smiled, taking the girls hand. "Let me see what we have he--"

-DEET DEET-

He frowned, letting out an annoyed grunt as he started shuffling in his pockets until he found his cell phone. He checked the name on its face, raising an eyebrow suspiciously. "Just one moment," he said to Abby, raising a finger to her then pressing the talk button and bringing it to his ear. "Chad?"

"They took her... you son of a bitch, was it you? Did you take her?" Chad yelled, clutching his head with both hands as he pressed the phone tight to his person.

Victor pulled the phone away from his ear as it squealed feedback, then returned it. "Chad? What are you talking about. I'm in LA. Who took who?"

"Koy! Who the fuck do you think, they took Koy! I came home from a game and they weren't here! I can't find them and the place is a mess and they're not here!"

"Okay Chad, okay... I'll be there soon. It's going to be okay... we're going to get her back, Chad. It's going to be fine."

Chad sobbed, but said nothing else until Victor disconnected the line.

He sighed, turning to Abby. His eyes were filled with pity. "I'm sorry... I hope that school was better at training you than I suspect they were."

Hunter got up from the bar and walked over to him. "What? What's going on?"

"Looks like our first round of training is going to be on-the-job."

CHAPTER 15

Salt Lake City, Utah

Chad woke up in Koy's bed clutching the lego giraffe-house so tight that the plastic was cracking under the strain. He was only faintly aware of when or how he had fallen asleep and for the briefest few moments of consciousness, he thought that he had dreamt everything that had happened last night.

Then he opened his eyes and realized where he was, and a cold lump immediately formed itself in his chest and worked its way up until it was in his throat. Fresh tears came and added to the ones that already soaked his sister's tiny blue pillow. He could smell her on it, that familiar scent that every person has, yet isn't noticed until they're gone. His lower lip curled in, turning his chin into a crumpled mess as he pulled the pillow into his face and wailed.

He cried for a full twenty minutes. He cried the way children cried, full out and loud and holding nothing back. He cried from every ounce of his being, from every pore and with every muscle.

When he stopped he released the pillow, which he'd held so tightly that there were now five half-moon indents on it. He clutched it to his chest as he sat up and shivered, his legs touching the floor as he tossed them over the side. With red, puffy eyes he looked around the room.

It was light out now but the sun wasn't facing the windows. It had to have been at least noon, perhaps even a little later. There were toys and clothes everywhere, but for the life of him he couldn't recall if he'd found it that way or if it was the result of his search for Koy. The floor underneath and around her closet was invisible, covered in mounds of her clothes that were still on their hangers.

He sobbed twice, then got up and walked out into the hall and to the top of the stairs. He saw the chunk that was missing from the wall again now. It appeared about fist shaped, and there were indeed three long scrapes coming down from it. His whole body shook at its sight and he kept going down the stairs.

When he got there his eyes went wide and his muscles went slack as something dawned on him for the first time. Something that should have long before, yet hadn't in his state of grief. He opened his mouth. When he spoke his words were whispered and dry, like a plea from a man caught in the middle of a sandstorm.

"Karen."

He dropped the pillow and ran out into Koy's playroom, his eyes scanning it frantically before he turned into the den.

His cards were scattered about and his table knocked over. There was a blanket stretched across the floor that had clearly been on the couch at one point but now lay in a bunched and violent mess. One of the end tables was knocked over, spilling nail polish and coke onto the hardwood.

"Karen!" he cried again, stepping over the blanket for some reason he couldn't quite calculate and out into the dining room. There was a chair overturned, its wooden backing cracked in two. He continued on into the kitchen again, spinning around three times as if very, very confused and finally collapsing into a little ball on the floor and holding his head as more tears came.

"Oh my God," a soft, feminine voice that for a moment he thought was Karen uttered. He felt a great swell of relief that he almost felt guilty for as delicate hands touched his shoulders, their warmth and meaning undeniable. He looked up quickly, his eyes filled with hope that was quickly dashed.

The girl was not Karen, not even close. She was taller than Karen and had long auburn hair and green eyes that were upturned now in pity as she looked directly at him, her hands holding him in a gentle but firm embrace. She smelled wrong, too. Karen smelled like fresh laundry. This woman had a very woodsy smell to her, like old pine.

"Are you alright?" Abby asked, her face filled with concern.

His chin crumpled again and he felt that horrid bulge in his chest, the fleeting relief bringing back all the emotions again as if they were new. He started to cry but managed to stop himself from wailing, his body choking out the urges in several raking sobs that shook him to the bone.

"Who are you?" he managed finally, his hair a tangled

mess that stuck to his damp cheeks.

"She's with me," came a gruff, solid voice.

He peered over Abby's shoulder and saw Victor standing in the doorway, still hanging open from last night. The porch was full of leaves that had blown in and something in the back of his brain was suddenly very concerned that a racoon had gotten in and that it would hurt Koy. That immediately reminded him that she was gone and his eyes welled up again and made his vision fuzzy.

"My name's Abby," she answered, as though Victor hadn't spoken for her. She shot him a glare from over her shoulder and then turned back to Chad, using one finger to push the hair out from his eyes. "Its okay. We're here to help."

Victor stepped into the porch and immediately bent over, examining the door knob. He reached out and jiggled it, first from the inside and then from the out. "It wasn't forced," he mumbled to himself, then called out. "Are your doors usually unlocked?"

Chad sniffed twice, raising his head from between his knees. He sniffed twice before he could answer. "No."

"They were allowed in," he said to himself, stroking the scruff on his chin.

Chad's face tensed again and he closed his eyes, leaning back against the wall and letting tears fall down his cheeks.

Abby rose to her feet and marched the few feet from where he sat to where Victor stood, just as he was standing up himself and coming into the kitchen. "Is that really necessary?" she hissed, trying hard not to let Chad hear.

"Not if we're just going to comfort him, no," he said,

looking her straight in the eye. "But if we're going to get his sister back? Then yes. Yes, it's very necessary."

"Could you at least pretend you know how he feels?"

His eyes had a spark in them when she said that, but not a pleasant one. There was a rage there that was barely tempered, his jaw going tight and his lips pursing. When he spoke it was crisply and cleanly, without any trace of the southern drawl that there was usually at least a hint of. "Actually, I do," he said, some of the anger fading already. He regained his composure, pulling his shirt down at the bottom to straighten it. "I know exactly how he feels."

She swallowed back as he walked past her, exhaling a deep breath through her nose that was full of redheaded fury. Like him she pushed it back, following him as he walked over to Chad.

As he bent down next to Chad in almost the same way Abby had, Victor's face lost all the anger it had embodied almost a moment ago. In fact it filled with pity and sorrow, his eyes upturning as he reached out to touch the man's arm but thought better of it. He looked like he was about to cry as well, but was much better at holding it back than Chad was.

Abby watched this interaction and felt a great swell of regret for what she had just said. She wasn't sure if Victor was simply better at handling pain than Chad... or if he'd just seen enough of it in his time to be able to control it a little better. She suspected it was actually both.

"It's going to be okay," he said, his voice oddly soothing. It sounded weird and out of place, yet comforting all at the same time.

Chad sniffed twice, opening his eyes and running a

hand back through his hair. "I didn't think you'd come."

"You called."

"I wouldn't have come."

"I said: Just call. Just call and your needs immediately come first. So, here I am."

Abby looked from one to the other.

Chad sniffed again, then coughed.

"It's going to be okay," Victor said one last time, his voice quiet now. He forced a smile wide enough to see under that haystack of scruff.

"Thank you," Chad said, his voice becoming small and sharp as tears found his cheeks again. He turned away from Victor and looked out the kitchen window, trying to control his breathing.

Victor stood up and started toward the hallway, taking a look at the toys scattered across the floor as he walked by them.

Abby took a step toward Chad and started to bend over to take his place, even though it looked as though he were off in another world with grief again.

"No," Victor said, neither harshly nor gently. "You're with me."

She stood back up and cocked an eyebrow at him. "Shouldn't someone stay with him?"

"He'll be fine," he frowned, turned to look at Chad for a moment. "He needs a minute."

She tisked, then stepped around Chad and over to follow Victor.

For a moment they both walked in silence, until they reached the foot on the stairs.

"I don't know what you think I'm going to do, anyway," she huffed, her hands in her pockets. "Do you think I've got some kind of trippy mystery-solving power or something?"

"No," he said, turning toward her. "But I'm assuming they taught you more at Port Haven than painting and fencing, correct?"

She paused, then nodded.

He gestured toward the stairwell. "Come on, then. We haven't got all day."

She paused, still hesitant for a moment, then started up the stairs.

She stopped at the hole in the wall, keeping her face turned forward. After a moment she turned to the left to regard it, the dull and dusty impact crater staring back at her sullenly. It was oddly shaped, round on the bottom and pointed on the top, forming a rudimentary teardrop shape. It had a small skid mark leading to it where paint had been worn off the wall. The hole itself was dotted with the white chalk of plaster and several log cracks that spider-webbed out from its epicentre.

"Somebody punch the wall?" Victor asked, coming up behind her one step at a time. He was moving slowly but wasn't examining anything along the way now... he was instead examining her as she examined things. There was a patience about him now, and even a small joy buried beneath the surface of his words, like a teacher watching a student put something they taught into practice.

"No..." Abby trailed, reaching out and gently trailing her index finger along the holes rough edge. It left its white powder on the ribs of her fingertip which fell to the stairs in tiny crumbs as she rubbed it back and forth against her thumb. "It wasn't a fist. It was her head."

He stepped up beside her now, standing on the stair under her and making them appear to be the same height. He leaned in over her shoulder and squinted to examine it himself, then turned and looked up the stairs. "Direction-ality is wrong if she was falling."

She turned and looked up as well, the top corner of Koy's bedroom door just visible beyond the bannister. "I don't think she fell."

"What do you think happened then?"

She clicked her tongue against the roof of her mouth a few times, holding her slender smooth chin in her hand and squeezing its flesh contemplatively. She leaned over the rail and stared out into the hallway, noticing Chad still curled on the kitchen floor.

"There were two of them," she said, and when she did she could almost see them. "At least two. Maybe more, but I don't think so."

"I concur."

"I don't think they were let in like you said. Maybe the door was unlocked accidentally or something, but I don't think they were let in. They came in through the kitchen and split off in two directions, one heading out the hallway here and the other one going through the din-ing room toward the living room."

Victor remained silent, watching her as her eyes moved back and forth in their sockets. He seemed to be enjoying simply watching her think.

"She heard them. I think... I think she heard the one that was heading out into the hall."

"Then what happened?"

"She ran out through this... play area over here," she said, waving her hand in the direction of Koy's play room. "She ran out and she saw one of the men going up the stairs. I think she tried to stop him or grab him or something, but the other one..."

"The other one was coming up behind her," he cut in, nodding.

"Yeah. He followed her out the same way she came in and grabbed her by the foot while she was on the stairs. Her forehead hit against the wall there and made that mark when she went down."

"I think she fought it even then," he added, cocking his head toward the dent. "Those three streaks coming down from the hole... fingernails?"

"Yeah... yeah," she sighed glumly. "She would have been face down on the stairs though with somebody on top of her... someone a lot bigger. I don't think the fight lasted very long."

In her mind she could see a large, muscular man with a shaved round head looming above Karen. His eyes had dark raccoon swirls under them and his skin was hard and leathery. He brought one of his massive fists up high above his head and then slammed it down on the base of her skull, driving her face into the stairs as well.

She winced at the thought.

"Come on," he said, motioning up the stairs. "There's more to see."

They continued up to the second floor slowly, keeping their footfalls as quiet as possible. There was something about the still of the house that made them feel the need to be still as well, as though something in the dark would know that they were there if they made too much noise. She'd felt it before once, on a hunting expedition with Jasper. After he fired a shot the entire forest had hushed instantly. Then just as now, she'd tiptoed her way to where she needed to be.

They stopped at the top of the stairs. The air up here was cool and crisp with fall, fresh on their skin and bringing them back to reality. At once Abby was swept up in the memory of Jasper again, sneaking up on her when she least expected it like it always did. She closed her eyes when she heard Victor behind her and for a moment she would have sworn the it was Jasper, taking off his coat and laying it gently around her shoulders.

He looked around for a moment, eying the mess that Chad had left the bathroom in, then craned his head to see around into Koy's room. "In here, I think."

She nodded without a word, swallowing hard. He stepped in front of her and walked into the room. She followed a moment later, a breeze propelling her from some forgotten open window.

She found Victor in the center of the room, squat down on the floor and examining a large footprint. There was a ray of light streaming in from the window that caught the dust in the air and became something almost solid as it shone a spotlight all around him. She watched him for a moment, then allowed her eyes to wander over the rest of the room.

There was a shelf on the wall across from her that had different stuffed toys on them of every type, shape and colour. They did not look dusty or even like they had been placed up there in any particular order or fashion, and she got the impression they were not just for show as they would have been in some homes. She could picture a little girl being tucked in to bed at night and picking which toys she would take to bed with her meticulously, thinking about each and every one before making her decision. Whoever was tucking her in would pack them around her, keeping her safe and warm all night in a bundle of furry friends.

Her clothes were sprawled out across the floor beneath her closet, most of them still on their hangers. There was a red felt dress near the top that stood out, looking like it had only seen the wash a few times. It was a Christmas dress, only worn once or twice a year. She pictured the girl smiling brightly when she walked downstairs with it on, holding Chad's hand and being excited to look pretty.

Abby suddenly felt it was wrong for her to be looking around the child's room. It felt voyeuristic and dirty. She curled her lip in disgust.

Victor looked up, then turned to look at her in his peripheral vision. He watched her like that for a moment, then frowned and turned back. He touched the dirt that someone's shoe had left, its clay imprint crumbling slightly under the pressure.

"Is it from them?"

"I don't think so," he frowned. "I think its Chad's."

She nodded, rubbing her bare arms with her hands as gooseflesh rippled through them all over.

He looked all around the room, stroking the stubble on his chin at first and then all the way down his neck. He had an oddly contemplative look on his face, his eyes falling over each item in the room individually and gauging its relevance.

"Why didn't Hunter come with us?" she asked finally, casting a glance back toward the door.

"Hunter had work elsewhere," he drawled, rising to his feet. "Lots of things going on... got a lot of plates spinning all at once."

"Have you been working with him long?"

"No," he responded curtly, brushing his hands on his jeans.

The comment took her aback, and she stammered slightly as a result. "No? I thought..."

"There's a lot going on, and I needed help. He's a friend of a friend... I don't know him that well."

"Oh..." she said, fumbling her fingers together near her waist. "I see."

He turned back to her and looked her up and down, from the top of her head to the bottom of her toes and back up again. They were as far apart as they could be in the room, yet he still felt it was too close when he looked at her like that. She shivered again, and this time it had nothing to do with the cold.

"You think a lot of him, don't you?" he asked finally, stretching a little before moving to examine the pile of clothes.

"Maybe," she stiffened. "You don't, obviously."

"I'll take my help where I can get it," he mulled, bobbing his head back and forth, as if weighing the pros and cons of different answers. "He lacks finesse. I don't think I'd have chosen him for this if I had any other options."

She opened her mouth to protest, then nodded slowly.

He turned to her again, seeing that she was distressed by what he had said. "I think he's going to be sticking around, though. After we clean up this mess, there's no real reason for him not too."

She nodded again, though was obviously still not convinced.

"What about your friend... Hunter mentioned something about another person at the school. Someone like you."

She huffed, touching her hands to her arms. "He's psychic, I think."

"Really?" he said, holding the E sound a long time and cocking his eyebrow into the air. It was the first time he had looked genuinely interested in anything since he'd picked her up in Los Angeles. "What makes you think that?"

"He knows things he shouldn't... but its not like he told me or anything. He never really tells me anything."

"People rarely do."

"What do you care, anyway?" she asked, squinting at him.

He turned away from her then, rubbing his thumb and forefinger together until the clay turned to dust and eventually drifted back onto the floor in tiny fragments of sediment. "We need all the help we can get."

"Help with what?" came a wet, sickly sounding voice.

The both of them turned to Koy's bedroom door and saw Chad there, his face stained a glimmering pink from his tears and his hair matted against his face. He had a sleepy, half-shut look to his eyes and looked feverish, although they knew that was not the case. There was a milky substance that looked partially solid in the corners of his lips.

"What happened?" Abby asked with genuine concern, taking a tentative step toward him.

"I threw up in the sink," he responded quietly. He frowned, paused, then spoke again. "Help with what?"

Victor turned to Chad, his eyes again filled with pity. There was a readiness to his posture, constantly on edge now as he spoke. "I'm trying to get together some people... some very special people. I have it on good authority that the world is going to need a group like this. Soon."

"People like me?" Abby asked, raising an eyebrow. "Is that what you mean? People like at Port Haven?"

"Yes," Victor said after a moment. He huffed out the word, clearly not wanting to have this conversation.

"And me?" Chad asked, furrowing his brow and pushing off of the door frame to stand on his own two feet. "You told me you were looking for talented people... what kind of talented?"

"There's time for all this later," he said, and it was not a request. "Right now we need to find the child."

Chad frowned at his avoidance of the question, but did not press it further. "You find anything that'll help?"

"No, but we already know who did this. I *warned* you that something like this would happen."

"Then why were we even looking?" Abby asked, cocking an eyebrow at him.

"Needed to make sure there was nothing here the police could use. If we could do this legally, it'd help," he mumbled, then turned to Chad and spoke up. "You haven't called the police yet, have you?"

"No..." Chad said, as if it took him a moment to re-member. "No, only you."

Victor nodded. "Good. It'll make things easier."

"Wait, what?" Chad spat, stepping toward him. "Make what easier? What do you think we're going to do here?"

Victor smiled. "It's okay. We'll get her back."

"What? How?"

He clapped a hand on Chad's shoulder and produced a smirk that was almost infectious.

CHAPTER 16

Los Angeles, California

He sat comfortably in a large chair, one that dwarfed both men in sheer girth. There was a bottle of wine in his right hand, a 1787 Chateau d'Yquem. He strummed his fingers along its edge rhythmically, almost obsessively, as he stared across the table.

Tony Chavez stood across from him and held his hat in his hands, wringing it back and forth like children did while being scolded in movies from the fifties. Sweat was running down his face in large glops, dripping from his chin and onto the floor.

"I find this very concerning," the man said, finally tipping up the bottle and pouring it into a tall glass. He brought it to his nose and then sniffed it lightly, swirling it in small, concentric circles. "To think that a man of your talents couldn't even handle a lone, unarmed girl."

"First, wasn't me," Tony corrected, raising a finger. "I sent Jon Bon and Logan to do it. Second, she wasn't alone. Had that crazy sumbitch with her, ripped a hole in the whole thing."

"I couldn't care less who she had with her," the man chuckled heartily, bringing the glass to his lips and having a long drink. He swished it between his cheeks for a moment, then swallowed and smiled. "I told you to either bring her to me or make her dead, and you haven't successfully done either. Twice now."

"Sir --"

"Arthur."

"*Arthur*," Tony corrected, rolling up his sleeves and revealing an arm full of colourful tattoos. "I think we might want to drop this one. I mean, in the grand scheme of things, what does it matter. She's gone. She wants nothing to do with any of this. Doesn't even know about any of this."

Arthur took another long swallow of his drink, then sighed. "Tony my friend, I believe we have stumbled upon the very reason you aren't burdened with an overabundance of intelligence."

Tony looked to be ready to say something in return, then stopped himself, and nodded.

"Just get it done," Arthur said, finishing the glass. "And make sure you let me know how it plays out."

Tony nodded, then turned and left the room.

CHAPTER 17

Salt Lake City, Utah

Karen woke up in the dark.

At first it was hard to tell the difference between when her eyelids were closed and when they were open, but eventually they caught hold to a faint strand of light and focused on it, growing accustomed until she could at least see a little. Even so, there wasn't much of a view. All she could see was the rough edge of a concrete wall, its painted gray surface as cold and desolate as it could be.

"Wher--" she started to say, but stopped immediately when dull pain throbbed violently through her jaw and down the base of her neck. Her head felt tight against her skin, as if her brain were trying to outgrow the confines of her skull. She ground her teeth and that only seemed to make it worse, amplifying the pressure at her temples a thousandfold. Even so, it was difficult to stop.

The floor she lay on was cold against her face, and she was faintly aware of a warm stream coming from her mouth that she hoped was simply drool. Her hands were bound behind her back, so tight that she couldn't even flex the muscles necessary to try and move. She couldn't feel her fingers, and there was a brief panic-stricken moment when she had to remind herself that they were there.

There was a sound near her, soft and quick. It almost sounded like a hiccup.

She tried to turn only to get a face full of gravel, then rocked her entire form and used the momentum to force her head around to look the other way.

Koy was sitting on a cot not far from her, her knees pulled up close to her face and held there tight by her slender arms. She sobbed twice more rapidly, rocking back and forth gently as she stared at Karen. Her eyes were bright and glistening with tears and fright.

"Koy?" Karen called, shuffling again to try and face her. The words hurt, the tone of them reverberating through her head and making her bruises ache even more. The more she woke up the more parts on her she found that hurt. She was becoming dimly aware that the flesh had been scraped off her knees. "Koy sweetie, are you okay?"

She sobbed, then started to cry again, burying her face into herself.

"Honey?" she said, trying to hide the fear in her voice and just sound soothing. "Honey shush, honey it's okay... Are you hurt? Hmm? Tell Auntie Karen what's wrong."

"Daytame inna woke meyup," she said, the words garbled through her child's dialect and a wealth of unshed tears. "Day woke meyup anna may me om ere anna no Tad!"

"I know, sweetie," Karen cooed, trying her best to comfort the child. The sound of the girl's pleas brought new tears to Karen's face as the memories of how she'd come to be here came flooding back. She winced, almost feeling the blow to the back of her head. "You're not hurt, are you?"

Koy nodded slowly.

"Where, honey? Where are you hurt?"

"Imma nee."

"On your knee?"

She nodded again, her lower lip sticking out and quivering heavily.

"Oh, Koy. That'll be okay. Okay?" she forced a smile, only then feeling how swollen her lip was.

"Kay," she said after a moment, sniffing. It was hard to tell if the sniffle was genuine or one of those things she did because she felt she was supposed to, but right now it didn't matter.

"Okay. Now, I need you to be a big girl and listen to me. I need you to come over here and help me up, okay? We have to get out of here, we have to get out of here right now, okay?"

Koy thought for a moment, then edged herself to the edge of the bed and nodded.

"Okay Koy, what I need you to do is --"

The metal snap of an old lock rang through the small walls, becoming larger than it was until it seemed to come from everywhere. Both girls turned to face the door with fear in their eyes, Karen twisting her neck painfully to do so. Koy's body went still, even her tiny chest stopped moving, her breath held tight in her throat. There was a long, painfully quiet moment as the both of them stared at the rusty edge of the door and waited for it to move.

After a moment Karen's lungs screamed for air and she took a deep breath, forcing a smile as she turned back to Koy. "Okay, what I need you to do is --"

The door opened and a large man entered wearing a tattered and stained blazer that looked as though it had been pulled out of a dumpster. The skin on his face and hands was ghostly white. Even the thick, throbbing veins that ran across the backs of his hands were pale. It made him look strange and alien. His eyebrows were shaved, but his hair was full and red.

"No!" Karen screamed, turning and trying to squirm. "You're not taking her! You're not!"

He reached out, his fingertips pudgy and calloused.

Koy screamed, long and shrill.

"No!"

He grabbed the rope that bound Karen's wrists and used it to pull her to her feet. She kicked and screamed and clenched her jaw, biting at the air around her.

"NO!" Koy screamed, but it wasn't as angry a cry as Karen had made.

He pulled her through the door and threw her to the floor. Her body bounced once and then skidded, scraping her hip clear to the bone before she slammed against the wall. Her eyes were closed again and her face slumped lazily against the floor.

"No, Kar, no!" Koy screamed again, getting up from the cot.

The man turned back to her, making eye contact with those dark gray pools of swamp water.

She stopped dead in her tracks. She brought her finger to her mouth and started to suck on it on reflex, as though

Chad had just stopped her from doing something wrong.

He stared at her for a long moment, then slammed the door behind him.

Koy stayed there for almost ten minutes, afraid to move. Eventually she turned back and laid down on the cot and started to cry.

CHAPTER 18

Salt Lake City, Utah

"Yeah!" Jackie Davis screamed, slapping the palm of his hand against the rickety plastic table he sat at.

He considered himself a fairly well educated man. He'd grown up in Skoke, Illinois and had always gotten straight A's, except in English Lit. He'd studied Engineering at Illinois College and had graduated in the top ten percentile, and was currently on the shortlist for a position at the Shane industrial lab in Los Angeles. He'd smoked pot but had never done anything harder. He'd quit smoking when he was nineteen and never looked back. He drank occasionally, but rarely in excess.

Despite all that, when Jasmine's panties hit the show room floor and she stretched one leg up to the top of the pole, all he could think to do was scream yeah and bang his hand against the table for dear life.

Cindy hesitated next to him, holding his drink a few inches above the table until it stopped shaking, then placed it on the clear surface with a slight sharp sound. "That'll be four ninety-five," she chirped, smiling as large as she could muster.

He reached into his pocket and took out a five, never once taking his eyes off the stage. She slid it into a small pouch on her side then dug her finger back in and fished about for change.

"Keep it," he said, neither politely nor impolitely, holding up his hand.

She smiled again and stepped away, heading back over to the bar. Only now did he actually look at her, his eyes dancing over her backside and focusing on the way the swell of her buttocks protruded from either side of her slender black thong. She felt his eyes on her as she walked away, staring at her until Jasmine spun her hair around again, bringing his attention back to the front.

She sighed, leaning her tray against the bar and slumping over it slightly.

"Rough time?" the bartender chuckled, looking up from the floor to smile at her as he stacked the bottom shelf of the fridge full of coolers.

"Getting there," she drawled. The smile she'd worked hard to plaster on was gone now, and it looked like she'd aged ten years in the past thirty seconds. She took a deep breath, then exhaled again, feeling the pressure on her chest as it hit the bar.

"Get that bitch in here!" came an urgent voice from behind her, and she nearly jumped out of her skin. She dropped her tray to the floor with a clang and her heart rate automatically doubled as she turned around, pressing her back tight against the bar. She knew that voice, had learned it well over the past week. She also knew that tone in it.

Brent stood in the doorway to his office, one hand laid on the metal rail of the stairwell. His face was drawn out and serious, and his frown was so deep that it looked as though it were trying to escape the confines of his face. His pupils were small beady holes in the center of his eyes, glaring straight ahead and burning a hole into whatever he was staring at.

Which, she realized after a moment with some relief, was not her.

She turned toward the stairwell as a large man shuffled his way out. He was so pale that she doubted he spent much time outside the club, so deprived of sunlight that he looked almost albino. She could only see his backside from here, even his arms disappearing around the front of his obese frame. He was inching forward and then lunging back over and over again.... forward, *lunge*, forward, *lunge*. With each lunge came a short scraping sound as something drew itself out against the side of the doorway. He grunted, ducked as far forward as he could, then gave one final lunge.

Karen finally pulled free from the doorframe, popping out with such unexpected force that he lost his grip on her shoulder. She fell to the hard tile floor, the side of her head connecting against it with an audible crack.

Cindy's mouth opened slightly as she turned from Karen's limp form to the bartender, who continued stocking his cooler. She looked over at Jackie Davis in the far corner who didn't appear to have heard anything, and she looked up at Jasmine, who didn't miss one beat of her routine. Finally, she turned back to Brent.

He wiped his nose in his sleeve, sighing impatiently

as the larger man bent over to grab Karen again, his fat fingers slipping repeatedly on her sweaty flesh. He picked her up twice more only to lose her again, her head slamming against the floor over and over.

Cindy winced with every impact.

"What the fuck is wrong with you? How the fuck you expect to ever pick up a woman if you can't even pick her up?" Brent barked, his tone jovial and yet mean. Hideously mean.

"I'm trying, boss," the man said, huffing angrily. Frustrated, he grabbed one arm with both hands and pulled. It was followed immediately by the slow, deliberate sound of something inside her stretching out to its physical limits and then cracking.

"Ah," Cindy winced, her face drawing down. She could almost feel it herself.

Brent turned to her, his head snapping tight from one direction to the next. "What the fuck is your problem?" he snapped.

"I... nothing, I..." she stammered, turning away from his steely gaze and kneeling down to pick up her tray. "I... I was just, um..."

"Will you get in here?" he barked again, turning back to the albino and pointing to the floor at his feet, in case the man didn't know where 'here' was.

He dragged her along the floor, her jeans making a long hissing sound scraping against the tile, until he made it to the stairs. He grunted, then bent over to gain some momentum and hauled her up. Her head took an odd angle, bending almost to the breaking point against the second stair as her shoulder wedged itself against the first.

He bent over, grabbed her, and repeated the process. He did this for all seven steps, and by the time he was done her shoulder looked like it might be dislocated and had taken on the colour of meat left out for too long.

Cindy ground her teeth more and more with every step, then again as Karen was dragged the last few feet into Brent's office and out of sight.

Brent continued to watch as the man did something in his office that caused a loud, uncomfortable shuffle, then turned back to the main floor. He watched Jasmine for a moment as she spun around the pole, then let his eyes fall to Cindy.

"Don't you have something to do?" he barked, straightening his shirt and rubbing his nose again.

"I -- yes, sorry, I..." she stammered again, looking around and trying her best to remember what should have been happening.

"Don't know why I pay these people..." Brent mumbled to himself, turning away from her and stepping back into his office.

He slammed the door behind him.

Cindy watched it for a long moment, staring at the plain wood as though expecting it to do something. She bit her lip, then turned back to the floor to see if Mr. Davis needed another drink.

CHAPTER 19

Salt Lake City, Utah

"And you actually think that'll work?" Chad asked, raising an eyebrow at Victor.

They'd made the trip to Janelle's Place in Victor's beaten up El Dorado faster than Chad ever had, with Abby in the back holding on to the seat for dear life. Both of them had questioned the intelligence of moving their conversation out of the house and into a more public forum, but Victor had insisted, stating that: 'stress made for stupid thinking.' Now he sat across from Chad, bushy blonde eyebrows raised but otherwise expressionless, sipping on a deep cup of coffee.

He stopped slurping, looking over the beveled rim at Chad. He lowered the cup slowly, wiped his mustache, then swallowed. "I do, actually. I think it's going to work out quite well."

Chad opened his mouth to retort, jutting his hand forward. Instead his mouth just hung open for a moment until he sighed, running both hands through his hair on either side of his head and staring down into his coffee.

Victor frowned, shaking his head.

"It is fairly out there," Abby agreed, leaning forward from her spot in the booth next to Victor. She was sipping on an iced hot chocolate through a straw and picking at the whipped cream on top with the nail of one index finger. "It depends on a lot of people acting in very specific ways. Like, ways that don't really make sense and that you couldn't know."

"Just because people *don't* know something, they assume you *can't*," Victor said in a matter-of-fact, fatherly tone. "But they can, and I do."

"How?" Chad asked, almost laughing. It got Sandi's attention in the corner. She held her gaze on him for a moment, waiting to see if he would look up and notice her, then turned away again. "How could you possibly?"

"I did the math," he said defensively, holding out his palms. He looked from Chad to Abby and then back again.

They both stared at him blankly. After a moment Abby turned away and slurped on her straw again and Chad threw his head back onto the chair. "I should've called the police..."

"No... no," Victor huffed, then forced a smile. It looked unnatural on his lips. "I swear to you, this will work."

"Why can't we just go in there?" he pleaded. "You're a big guy. Lets go in and bust up the place."

"Yeah," Abby agreed, letting out a little laugh. "What could they do? Call the police and say we beat them up and took the kid they kidnapped?"

"Trust me, this will work," Victor said, calming himself and grabbing his mug again, taking a sip. "I've been doing this a long time. This will work... and if it doesn't, we can still do it your way."

Chad cocked an eyebrow. "You swear?"

"What?"

He pursed his lips, speaking slowly. "Do you *swear* that if this doesn't work, you'll do it my way? You'll just go in with guns blazing and take care of this? You'll do that for me?"

Victor paused, setting down his cup again and looking him directly in the eye. "Yes."

Chad let out a sigh of relief, a smile perking over the corners of his lips for the first time since he woke up.

"Yes, of course," he repeated, as if amused by the notion. His tone seemed to relax Abby as well, her shoulders loosening visibly next to him. "I'll do whatever it takes. I'm at your disposal. But we might as well do this the easy way first... and if this goes according to plan, it will be easy."

"It won't go according to plan."

"It will."

"It can't."

"But it will."

Chad huffed, then went back to drinking his coffee.

"I'm not sure what I'm supposed to be doing during all this," Abby grimaced, picking at the white froth on top of her drink. "I have no idea how to do what you're asking me to do."

"That's part of the point, actually," Victor winked. "You'll do fine. You'll both do fine."

"If that guy lays a hand on me, I'm just gonna belt him."

"He won't... everything will be fine."

She paused. "You're fairly proud of yourself right now, aren't you?" she smirked, pointing at him.

"Yes," he said, then continued to mull the question over before speaking again. "Yes I am, actually."

Northton, Idaho

"Mary?" Lucas called, tapping twice on his daughter's bedroom door. He was silent for a moment, scratching the stubble on his chin as he awaited a response. He gave about thirty seconds, then knocked again. "Mary?"

After another seconds pause he opened the door and stepped through. The room was vacant, quiet and still, an eerie thickness in the atmosphere of it. For the first time in almost a decade he took a breath in her room without getting a snootfull of hair spray or perfume or incense. While his nostrils were thankful for this fact, the rest of his body became stressed and he immediately began to perspire.

He'd heard other fathers speak of a bond between their daughters and themselves... a form of intuition bordering on psychic that told them when their children were in danger. At first he'd laughed about it, thinking those men to be gullible idiots. Then as more and more said the same, he began to question his effectiveness as a parent. Perhaps there was some genetic blueprint for fatherhood that he was missing? It had been a source of guilt for him for some time. He'd tried to cover it, to do all the things a good father should and more... but he'd secretly always wondered if Mary felt it, too. Wondered if it affected her on some level, or that it would now that she was so close to adulthood.

Tonight, his fears on the matter were alleviated, replaced with new ones. Worse ones.

He felt his stomach do a backflip and acid rise in his throat and he knew... just knew that his daughter was in trouble. That she was in pain. That she was hurt. "KIM! he screamed, turning from the room and running down the stairs, "Call the Sheriff! Call Luke and Brian!!

"Something's happened to MARY!!"

CHAPTER 20

Salt Lake City, Utah

Victor's El Dorado had a stale smell of indeterminate origin that was barely covered by the pine freshener that hung from his rearview mirror. It was not the type of odour that one got used to after a few moments either, causing Chad to wrinkle his nose in disgust well over an hour after he got in.

"What the hell is that?" he asked finally, turning to Victor in the driver's side as he clacked his tongue against the roof of his mouth. The stench was so powerful that he was convinced he could *taste* it.

"Hmm?" Victor asked, tilting his head toward Chad but keeping his eyes trained on the long stretch of pavement in front of the car. His hands gripped the steering wheel in front of him at ten and two even though the motor was off, so tight that his knuckles were white. "What's that?"

"The smell, man... what's that smell?"

"I... I don't know," he replied, as though not really sure what he'd even been asked. He raised a hand briefly for quiet. "Shush. She's almost there."

About a hundred metres ahead of them, Abby finally reached the back entrance of *The Pearl Necklace* and
knocked twice. She looked tiny alongside the large gray
metal door, and for a moment a wash of mild panic fluttered over Victor and settled in the center of his chest.

"Come on..." he whispered to himself, twisting his
hands over the wheel. "Come on..."

The door opened after a moment and a man with dark
complexion that was about his size opened the door. He
recognized him instantly as the dealer, Sigmund, from
the last time he was there. He looked down at Abby, then
around her, as if surprised that she was there on her own.
Finally he said something to her, something short.

"Can you hear what they're saying?" Chad whispered,
unable to take his eyes from the girl as well. "Is that one
of your powers?"

"No," he said, watching as Abby nodded twice. He
could tell she was smiling somehow, the way she bobbed
on her feet. The man laughed, shrugged his shoulders,
then stepped aside and let her in. He turned to Chad, his
nose crinkled as if just realizing what he'd been asked.
"She's in. She's fine... What?"

"What can you do... or, what do you think we can
do?"

"I'm not sure about her," he admitted, frowning. He
paused a long time, then added. "Her friend is a telepath...
I don't *do* anything."

"Bullshit."

"No, really."

"Then why would you..."

"The world is a mess, kid," he said, turning to look at him. "It's not going to get better on its own."

Chad frowned, then looked to acknowledge this. He turned back to the door, waiting to see if Abby would come right back out. She did not. "What about me?" he asked finally, his voice full of trepidation. "What do you think I do?"

Victor paused, still looking at the door from over his knuckles.

"Well?"

He opened his mouth, then closed it, then opened it again. "I think you're lucky."

Chad stared at him for a long moment, as if waiting for him to say he was joking. "You're... serious."

"The technical term is low-level probability control. You bend odds in your favour. Unconsciously of course, but I think with time... I think I could help you develop it."

Chad stared at him, then let out a breath and laughed. After a moment he stopped, wiped his nose, then started again. It wasn't sarcastic or spiteful, just the full on belly laugh of someone so at the end of their rope that they could do nothing else.

"What's so funny?" Victor asked, after waiting for Chad's laughter to subside.

"*That* was funny. That, what you just said. Me, lucky. Chad Matthews, the luckiest man alive."

"I see."

"Because let me tell you," he said, turning back to Victor with his nose curled up in disgust. His eyes were filled with tears and hate. "If you knew one god damned thing about my life, you wouldn't say that."

Victor pursed his lips and nodded.

Chad turned back toward the front of the car, sniffed twice, then composed himself in silence.

"For example?" Victor asked after a moment, trying to make his gruff voice as calm as he could, turning to face Chad.

"What?" he asked, surprised.

"Can you give me an example of this so-called 'un-luckiness'?"

"Right now doesn't count?"

"No... as horrible as this is, this isn't happening to *you*. It's happening to your sister and your friend. That said, and don't take this the wrong way, but perhaps it *wouldn't* have happened if you'd been there. Maybe simply you being present at your home would have meant that they tripped on the stairs. Or that they wouldn't have even been able to find the place."

"Okay," Chad snapped, his lip curling with spite yet still seeming a little happy that he was about to get the upper hand. "Okay, I got you. Six months ago, my parents die in a car accident. Right in front of me my Dad bled out with a big honkin' piece of metal sticking out of his face. Lucky, huh? Lucky."

"Mmm. That is bad," Victor agreed, clicking his lips together and turning back to the road. "Read about that when I found out about you. Said you were actually in the car, right?"

Chad paused, staring at him for a long moment. He wanted Victor to turn and look at him, but he didn't. "Yeah."

"Koy too?"

"....Yeah."

"Paper said there wasn't a scratch on either one of you. Said the car had been totalled and that the cab had bent around you. That if you'd been anywhere else in the car or if your dad had been going even a mile faster you both would've been killed. Said it was a miracle."

"Yeah."

"Did you see it coming? The accident I mean."

"Only a second before."

"And what did you do? Did you call out to your Dad? Try to get him to stop?"

"No, I... I just jumped for Koy. I didn't have my seat belt on and I moved over her to protect her. With my body."

"So if I'm right... the only reason your sister survived was because you were preventing anything from getting to her."

Chad did not respond.

Victor turned to face him finally, locking eyes with him. "That seems pretty damn lucky to me."

Chad stopped, taken aback, then turned back toward the front and remained silent. They stayed like that for several minutes, neither man speaking or acknowledging the other in any way. Chad broke the silence eventually, though his voice was small and far away. "When do you think you should go in?"

"Now," he replied curtly, opening up the door without looking at Chad and stepping out. "Give it five minutes, then raise hell."

Chad nodded, though Victor didn't see it. He slammed

the door to his El Dorado then started the short walk to the back entrance of the strip club.

Victor walked up to the large metal door at the back entrance to *The Pearl Necklace* and frowned, casting a glance from side to side. He looked down at the black corduroy shirt he was wearing and brushed a healthy sample of dirt off the midsection. He took a deep breath, puffed out his cheeks, then exhaled.

"The things I do," he sighed to himself, then took out his phone and flipped it to the keyboard, punched in a few words, then put it back in his pocket. Raising a clenched fist, he knocked three times.

There was a metal snap inside almost immediately and Sigmund opened the door again, producing a long whine of rusted metal. He stopped, looked at Victor for a long moment, then smiled. "Didn't think you'd be back."

"What can I say?" he laughed, forcing a broad smile. "I'm a glutton for punishment."

Sigmund laughed, stepping aside to let Victor in. "How'd that thing with your missus go?"

The door shut behind them.

Chad watched from the car. He took a deep breath then opened the door, leaned out, and threw up.

Chad stormed up to the strip club door, his brow furrowed and angry. His job was easier than the others. While Abby and Victor had to pretend to be pleasant, rational people, he had to be angry. To be so out of his mind with rage that he would do anything.

It wasn't much of a stretch at this point.

With every step he took his anger and fear and adrenaline amplified upon itself, becoming stronger and stronger until he suspected he might vibrate out of his own skin.

He raised his fist and slammed on the door three times.

There was no answer at first, and with every second that passed his breath became heavier and heavier while his face became redder and redder. His stomach did a flip inside his gut and for a second he was worried he might throw up again, but he forced it back and then knocked three more times.

"Come on you fuckers!" he bellowed at the top of his lungs. "I know you're in there!"

He fumed, his nostrils so large they felt like they'd just pushed out golf balls. There was still silence, and it occurred to him that he might have overplayed his hand. A brief but powerful fear tingling over him, replacing the anger.

Then the latch snapped to the side and turned, the door swinging in and revealing the same man that had been so cheery to Victor a moment ago. His face was stern now, his brow down low and forming a hard line over his eyes. "What did you just say?" he asked, his voice low but booming.

"Fuckers!" Chad screamed, lunging toward the door. The man put out an arm to stop him, and even then he tried to claw and kick his way through until he was eventually pushed back. "You goddamnfuckers! I'll kill you, you understand me? I'll fucking kill you!"

"All right, that's enough out of you," he sighed, holding his palm against Chad's chest to keep him back. "You gots to go."

"You can't stop me!" he screamed, his face almost to the point of tears again. "You can't! You understand me? That's my sister! You're going to die you fat fucking god damn --"

"Hey," came a hard, quick tone.

Chad pushed away from the doorman, now able to see past him and into the door frame.

Brent stood there, his broad shoulders pulled back straight and almost stretching from one end of the doorway to the other. He was dressed up in what Chad assumed was one of his best suits, a deep navy blue with white pinstripes. His face was void of all emotion, regarding Chad with those tiny black eyes of his. He was squinting slightly, but it was hard to tell with the heavy bags that formed each eyelid. He looked like he hadn't slept in days.

Chad's muscles seemed to relax under the man's glare, his arms falling to his sides.

"There now," Brent chuckled. "Is that so hard? See, I can be reasonable if you can. What can I do for you?"

"You took my sister, you fucker," Chad snarled, his upper lip curling like a dogs and showing his teeth all the way to the gums.

"I did," Brent smiled, patting something in his breast pocket. "I find sometimes men of good character require... motivation to do the right thing. To choose the right path. You needed me to move you, Mr. Matthews. To motivate you into the right choice. You need to come and work for me."

"I'm not going to come work for you," Chad spat indignantly, looking Brent up and down. "I'll *never* come work for *you*, do you understand me?"

Brent watched him for a second, then nodded. A wry smile spread over his lips. "Okay."

Chad stopped, raising an eyebrow. "Okay?"

"Okay. I can see you're a man of principle. That you're not going to roll over just because I poke at you with a sharp stick... tell you what, come in here and we'll talk it over."

Chad hesitated, then stepped in. Sigmund closed the door behind him, latching it with a sharp snap that made Chad jump.

The hallway was long and dark, with only one bulb sticking out from the wall in its center to light the whole thing. The distant scurry of creatures that lived low to the ground could be heard all around, their squeaks and chirps just barely audible above the sound of the bass speakers upstairs. The ceiling shook as people with thick-heeled boots walked about on drunken legs, sending bits of dust down through the cracks and into Chad's hair.

"If you think I'm going to leave here without my sister, you're fucking crazy," he said, not bothering to turn and look at Brent as they stepped along side by side toward the end of the hallway.

"Oh, I wouldn't suggest that... I can tell when a man's made up his mind," he smiled smugly.

"Well, what then?"

"I've got a game going on tonight," Brent said, putting both hands into his pockets as though he were a man going for a stroll in the park. "More players than usual, seven now including me, to be exact. The buy in is three grand a piece, but the winner doesn't get the money."

Chad turned toward him, a confused look on his face.

"The winner gets to give *me* the money, in exchange for your sister."

Chad's face turned white. "Are you suggesting I... *play* you for her?"

"Well, not *just* me," Brent chuckled. "But yes, that is the gist."

Chad shuddered noticeably.

"Do we have a deal?" Brent smiled, extending a hand.

He looked at it for a second, clenched his teeth, then took it and pumped twice. "Deal."

Brent nodded, the motioned toward the door at the end of the hall. Both men started toward it.

"Doesn't seem like a great deal, though," Chad mused, a suspicious tone to his voice. "I mean, the whole reason you took her is because you couldn't beat me."

"Maybe I just want my money back?" Brent beamed. "I'm not an unreasonable man."

He eyed him for a long moment. "Sure," he drawled, just as he opened the door.

The light here was bright compared to the dark of the hallway, and Chad found himself squinting for a moment to get used to it as Brent brushed past him.

It was the same room that it had always been, but the table was different now. It was larger to accommodate the extra players and the felt on it was a royal hue of purple instead of green. It made the whole room seem darker somehow, more gloomy. There was still that light in the center though, shining down on the cards and chips already divvied out and making them glimmer.

Brent stood by a comfortable looking chair at the far side of the table, motioning to an empty seat just to his right.

"You saved me a spot?" Chad asked, frowning.

"I had a hunch you'd be coming."

Chad did not respond, simply walked around the table and took his place.

On the other side of Brent, Sigmund took his place. He'd walked up behind the both of them so silently that Chad hadn't even realized he was there.

He took the new deck of cards out of the center of the table and slid the cards out, removing both jokers and one card explaining the rules of poker. Strumming his thumb across the bridge of them, he filled the room with a smell that at any other time would have made Chad smile.

Tonight it made him sick.

To the dealer's left, scrunched right up to the table and almost bumping elbows with his, was Abby. Her auburn hair had been drawn up with an elastic and held out of her face. Her green eyes sparkled in the light as she played with her chips, flipping them back and forth between her fingers. After a moment she looked up at him and they shared a brief glance before he looked away, trying their best to avoid eye contact. Still, it was long enough for those eyes to have an effect on him, and some primal, masculine urge in the back of his mind could not help but think that, if the situation were different, he might have had to try out Victor's 'good luck' theory on her.

A tall man named Joseph wearing thick rimmed glasses and a pasty expression sat next to her, his eyes jolting in the direction of Abby's breasts. He was wearing an orange plastic rain catcher that had the sleeves rolled up to the elbows and looked as though he'd stepped straight out of an eighties porno. He was chewing on the inside of his own mouth almost compulsively, and smelled like he'd rolled around in marijuana before coming in.

Next to him and across from Brent was Victor, who sat with his elbows on the table and his fingers laced together in front of his face. Only his eyes were visible, and even they were partially obscured by his hair.

There was an Indian man next to him named Hasheem that was wearing a leather jacket that looked to cost more than everyone else's wardrobe combined. He was chewing gum and his eyes were moving from one player to the next, staring them directly in the eye and trying to be intimidating. For the most part, he was succeeding.

Between Hasheem and Chad was an older man named Clyde with receding red hair that revealed a scalp full of liver spots, thick-rimmed glasses and a busy mustache. He had his hands laid on the table in front of him and stared at them intently.

Finally, a woman came in wearing a cheap black dress that Chad thought was Cindy at first, but when he looked he saw that it wasn't.

"That's Jasmine," Brent said, motioning to the girl and smiling.

Her name on his lips seemed to make the girl shudder.

"Just ask her if you need anything to drink," he said,

turning from his empty cup holder and then to her. When he spoke again his voice wasn't nearly as warm as it had been to that point. "Which I do, by the way."

She nodded, stepping out of the beam of light to get a glass.

Brent stared across the table at Victor, who met his gaze unwaveringly. "I didn't expect to see you here again."

"You know what they say," he said, shrugging his massive shoulders. "You can't keep a good horse down."

"Hn," he grunted, then frowned and addressed the table. "Okay gentlemen, this is a very special night. The game is no-limit hold 'em, your buy ins have already been taken by Jasmine to the front desk. The game continues until only one remains, no matter how long that takes. There are no buy backs tonight. You have your chance, people. Any questions?"

The table was silent.

"Let's begin," he said, pulling out his chair and sitting down.

As the dealer shuffled the cards, Chad bit his lip, then leaned over toward Brent and whispered. "You don't need my money?"

"I know you're good for it," he soothed, motioning the thought away. "Besides, we expect you to win anyway, right?"

Chad nodded and turned back to the table.

The dealer tossed a card down face up in front of Abby. It was the ace of spades. "What's this?" she asked, staring down at it.

"First Jack deals," he explained.

"Ah..." she trailed.

Victor shot her a sideways glance.

"... We don't play that way where I'm from."

He shrugged, then continued to deal, handing Joseph a deuce of diamonds and Victor a king of hearts. Hasheem got another king, this one of spades, and Clyde got a seven. When he got to Chad he tossed up his card and flicked it. It landed just in front of his stack of chips, its one eye glaring right at him.

"Jack of clubs," the dealer stated, motioning with his fingers for the cards to be returned to him before handing out the dealer, big blind and small blind tokens.

"Lucky," Victor said under his breath.

Chad shot him a look.

The dealer handed out two cards each, starting with Brent and ending with Chad. Brent grabbed a single red chip and tossed it forward into the center of the table. He turned to Abby, who peeled back the corner of both her cards to peek at them, then placed them side by side. She had a seven and a six of clubs.

After a moment Chad coughed and she looked up, realizing that everyone was staring at her.

"What?" she asked, looking around.

"Big blind," Brent said coldly, but with a sly grin at the side of his mouth. "You're the big blind. You owe in two reds before we start anything."

"Oh!" she chirped, an embarrassed expression on her face as she winced and clenched her teeth. She shot a glare at Victor as she tossed in the chips. "That's not how we play where I'm from, either."

Brent chuckled, looking her up and down and paying special attention to the cusp of her vee-necked blouse.

"Usually I don't like to see new faces... but with a face like yours, I'll make an exception."

She swallowed, gave him a polite smile, then turned to glare at Victor again.

"Where *are* you from anyway? You here in town?"

"No... no. I'm out from California."

"California?" he smiled, even as Joseph tossed his cards back to the dealer. "No shit. I know California. What part?"

"Port Haven," she frowned.

Victor nodded at her, then tossed in two reds.

"I'm not familiar with any place called Port Haven..." he droned, still looking her up and down with his beady little eyes.

"You wouldn't be," she smiled smugly, leaning her cheek down against the heel of her palm. "It's a school."

A hush fell over the table as Hasheem put in his two red chips. Each man looked at each other, then between Abby and Brent.

"Hnnn," Brent laughed from between clenched teeth, humming to himself, then turned to Clyde. "It's a school, she says."

Clyde snickered, and then the others laughed as well.

Abby beamed.

Clyde folded his cards.

Chad picked up his and stared at them. The first was a deuce of hearts, the second a three of clubs. He frowned, then threw them away.

"Everyone's starting out conservative, huh?" Brent laughed, grabbing a handful of chips and tossing them into the center. They rolled and bounced about until each found their place on the felt. "Can't have that. Five hundred."

Hasheem huffed, puffing out his cheeks.

Abby stared at the chips on the table, counting them mentally, then picked up an equal number and tossed them in without a word.

Victor looked at her, then smiled. "You have no idea how much you just put in, do you?"

She blushed. "Nope. I just matched colour for colour."

All the men laughed but Brent, who rolled his eyes impatiently.

"I'm in," Victor said finally, taking a single black and throwing it in.

Hasheem nodded, also throwing in a black chip.

The dealer nodded, burned one card and put it aside, then placed three cards on the table in a row. The ace of hearts, the two of diamonds and the king of spades.

Brent stuck out his lower lip. "Check."

"Check!" Abby said.

Victor tapped the table twice with one finger, as did Haseem.

Another card was burned, then the turn was laid. The nine of hearts.

Brent strummed his thumb along his lips, then grabbed two blacks and threw them in. "One thousand."

Abby took two blacks and threw them in.

Victor sighed, pulling up the ends of his cards. He had pocket eights. "That's painful," he grumbled, tossing them away.

Hasheem took two blacks from his pile and put them

in.

The final card joined the other four: another nine, this one of diamonds.

"Well. That changes things, doesn't it?" Victor laughed.

Brent frowned, then placed a chip on the pile. "Five hundred."

"Fold," Abby said, almost in a happy voice. She placed her hands in front of her patiently and turned to Hasheem.

He looked at his cards a moment, then nodded. "All in," he said, his accent more Maryland than Arab.

Brent's face drew out into a white-toned frown as Hasheem pushed his chips in. "Bit early for stuff like that, ain't it?" he growled.

Hasheem shrugged, then smiled.

"Call," Brent smirked, then tossed up his cards. He had an ace of spades and a king of diamonds.

Hasheem stared at them a long moment, then slammed his knuckle against the table. "Fuck!" he exclaimed.

"Take it that means you don't have the cards?"

Hasheem did not respond, just grabbed his coat from the back of his chair and stormed out the way he came. A moment after the door closed they heard a loud thud of a fist slamming sheet metal, then nothing again until the door opened to the outside. They paid attention to nei-ther.

"Well, that was rude," Brent chuckled, raking in his chips as the dealer started to take the cards back.

Chad picked up the cards to hand them to him, glanc-ing at them as he did. He'd had the king of hearts and a deuce of clubs.

At the end of the first hand, Brent Joby had almost nine thousand dollars worth of chips and his closest competitor was Chad, who still had just his original three thousand.

Chad shot Victor a look.

CHAPTER 21

Salt Lake City, Utah

Koy lay with her head against her cot in the dark, trying hard not to let her imagination get carried away with her.

Chad had always told her she had too much of an active imagination, always imagining things in the dark. That they were just make believe. But she could hear them. She was sure of it.

She buried her head so deep into the hard mattress that her nose hurt, and tried hard not to look at the demons in the dark. After a long, tense moment, she cried out.

"Tad?" she wailed, her voice wet and broken.

When nobody answered, she tried her best to go back to sleep.

∞

Abby let out a worried sigh as her second card was handed to her, looking down at them as though they'd betrayed her. She picked them up, looked at them, then laid them back down. One was an ace, the other a king. She watched as all the men put out their blinds, circling all the way around the table and finally ending up back at her. "Call," she said, putting in four red and nodding.

The dealer laid three cards, the two of diamonds, the eight of spades and the five of diamonds.

Next to her, she heard Joseph swish spit back and forth in his mouth, then grab chips.

"Four hundred," he said, as evenly as he could.

Victor looked down at his cards, a queen-five off suit combination. "Double that," he huffed, tossing out a black and three reds.

Clyde cursed under his breath, looking from the flop to his cards and then back again. He cursed again, grabbed a stack of reds and threw them in.

Chad folded.

"You're not even gonna try, are you?" Brent laughed, elbowing him. After a moment his face became serious. "You should have a drink. It'll soften the blow."

Chad squinted at him, but said nothing.

He sneered, then folded himself.

Abby frowned, then put in her eight hundred.

Joseph folded.

The dealer licked his finger and flipped up a card, looked at it himself, then placing it aside. He then turned up another and placed it with the others. It was a six of spades.

"Well," Joseph mumbled, tapping the table. "*That* didn't help anybody."

Victor looked down at his pile, which now composed of a single red chip. He smiled, then shrugged. "All in."

"But I've been wrong before."

"Fuck," Clyde said again, then put in his hundred.

"Did it hurt you that much?" Victor laughed.

He glared.

Abby put her last chip in. "That's all I have," she snorted.

"That's all for the betting," Brent smiled. "They're both all in."

The dealer turned up the last card, the jack of diamonds.

Victor snorted, turning over his. "Was bluffing. Wasn't even a smart one. All I've got is a pair of fives."

Clyde smirked, turning his cards over one at a time. He had a ten and a queen of diamonds. "Diamond flush."

Abby looked at his cards and furrowed her brow. "Well, if that's good..." she started, flipping over her ace-king. "Shouldn't this be better?"

Victor laughed, slapping the table.

They were both of diamonds.

Clyde stared at them a moment, then cursed again.

"Two more out," Brent chirped, watching as Victor stood. He turned to Abby. "You just might end up lucking your way into this, doll."

As Chad watched Victor leave, he felt the sweat on the back of his neck become prominent and trickle down in a little stream.

Victor looked at him as he left, giving him a wink as the dealer shuffled the cards again.

"Okay!" Brent said, his tone much happier now, clapping his hands and then rubbing them together. "Now it's a game of poker."

The dealer handed out the cards again and Chad slapped his hand down on them, pinning them to the table for a moment before turning them up. They were the seven of hearts and the deuce of clubs. "Pfft," he hissed, tossing out his small blind, then mumbled. "Thought I was supposed to be lucky."

Abby looked up at this, a concerned look on her face.

"Everyone's luck runs out sometime," Brent grinned, peeking at his cards and putting out his big blind as well.

Abby frowned, staring at Chad for a moment before turning down to her pile of chips and pushing them all forward. "All in."

"Puh!" Brent gasped, taking a mouthful of his drink.

Joseph looked at his cards, nodded, then pushed his chips forward as well.

Chad shook his head, picking up his cards to throw them away. When he did he caught Abby's eyes and stopped. They were pleading with him, practically wet with desperation. He paused, then put his cards back down and took a deep breath. "All in," he sighed, pushing his chips forward.

"Apparently someone knows something I don't," Brent groaned, tossing away his cards.

Joseph turned up his cards. Pocket nines.

Abby smirked happily and flipped hers over, revealing pocket aces. "Even I know they're good."

Chad frowned, then turned his own over.

Joseph laughed. "That's the worst hand in poker. What the fuck you thinkin'?"

He looked at Abby, folding his hands across his mouth. "Had a feeling."

The dealer laid out the flop, consisting of an ace a five and a deuce.

"Guess that does me in," Joseph drawled.

The next card came, another deuce.

Chad perked up his ears.

The last came... a seven.

"A full house," he said quietly, staring down at the table in disbelief.

Victor paused to organize his thoughts, taking another step forward. "I simply want to know: do you have any idea what the chances of you winning that hand the way you did are?"

Chad stared at him quizzically for a moment, as still as a picture with one eyebrow raised. "No," he said finally, his posture relaxing just a little but still very on edge. "What difference does it make?"

"The odds are astronomical. At least three hundred to one if my math is right, and it always is."

"Jesus," Joseph huffed, finished his drink in one gulp, then turned and left. "Fucking goddamn Jesus."

Abby smiled at Chad as his chips were pushed forward. His jaw was still slack.

CHAPTER 22

Salt Lake City, Utah

Cindy leaned against the bar for just a moment, letting its solid smoothness brace her weight and let out a deep breath. Her hair dangled down against her cheeks, just touching her shoulders and tickling them as the air conditioning pushed it from side to side.

She'd been working nearly ten hours in four inch heels, and thought her lower back might actually snap in two at any given moment if she didn't get a break soon.

"Hard night?" the bartender asked, smirking at her. His hair was cropped short and made the rest of his head look just a little too big for it, but other than that he wasn't difficult on the eyes. He seemed to have a boyish charm that she'd long suspected wasn't anything more than superficial nicety, but had never found out for sure.

She winced, then smiled slowly and nodded.

"How's that kid back in the corner doing? He still giving you trouble?"

"Naw, he calmed down after the third drink. The alkies always do, once you get their alcohol-blood levels back up to par."

"Ha. Yeah," he chuckled, averting his eyes for an instant.

Her head turned to one side, the slight twitch the only sign of her interest in what had just happened. "Can you get me a water or something? This job is gonna kill --"

Victor grabbed her by her shoulder and spun her around, sending her tray falling to the floor. It landed there with a loud clang, drawing the attention of all the patrons near the bar. "Where is she?" he barked, with a scowl so full that his face had drawn gutters on either side of his nose.

"Hey!" the bartender snapped, rising to his feet and taking Victor by the arm.

He turned and looked at the much smaller man, his eyes going narrow. "You're a closet alcoholic and a closet homosexual," he said crisply.

The man stopped, releasing Victor and opening his mouth in shock.

"Neither of which you are terribly efficient in hiding. Touch my arm again, and you'll lose a finger," he turned back to Cindy without waiting for a response, locking his eyes onto hers. "Where is she?"

"I --" she stammered, sandwiched between him and the counter that had brought so much relief a moment ago. "I don't know what you're talking about."

He slammed his hand against the counter.

She jumped.

"You know damn well what I'm talking about! The girl! Where did they bring the girl?"

Her lip quivering, she forced herself to look away

from those piercing eyes that seemed to be dissecting her right down to the hallows of her soul. "I can't... I need this job."

"What you need is to grow a backbone," he snapped. "Or do you intend to spend the rest of your life here, feeling bad about yourself and sucking coke off your boss' dick for a few extra dollars an hour?"

Her mouth opened and her eyes watered. She tried to make words, to fire something back... but nothing came. Finally, she managed: "How?"

"The same way I know how you got here. About the boyfriend back home in Bumfuck Nowhere, USA. He used to treat you like crap, didn't he? Sure he did. He didn't mean to, though. I'll bet he seemed sweet at first."

"No, I --"

"And you'd sit there in the backseat of his car while his fingers fumbled about clumsily and you'd think about your escape. About making it out and making it big. But that same timid smile that he brought out in you with every backhanded remark kept you from getting noticed. By the boys, by the employers..."

"Stop."

"And then you came here. And that son of a bitch hurts you the way he does, and you don't deserve it. But you think you do, and that's all anyone like him ever needed. Slip his cock in through that crack and pump you full of even more self doubt."

She stopped trying to interject now, her eyes having found some null space on the floor to stare at.

"But here's the plot twist: you can turn this back on him. Unless, you *want* to stay here."

infinity

She looked back up at him, her eyes fuming but full of expectation.

"Where's the girl?"

She nodded, then picked up her tray and started toward the stairwell. He followed less than a foot behind her, and when they reached the first step she summoned her courage and turned to face him. "He wasn't my boyfriend. He was just... just a boy. Someone I liked. That didn't like me."

"All the worse then," he sighed empathetically.

"How did you *know* all that?"

He smirked.

CHAPTER 23

Salt Lake City, Utah

Chad and Brent stared at each other from across the table, their features turned into shadowy blotches under the light hanging above.

The dealer was gone now, and Abby and Jasmine stood with their backs against the far wall and watched.

The deck lay between them on the table, like a loaded gun waiting to see who would be fast enough to draw it first.

After several tense moments, Brent allowed a playful grin to slip through his otherwise impenetrable demeanor. He reached for the deck, gripped its edges gently between his thumb and forefinger, and slid them over to rest in his shadow.

"I was kind of hoping it would come down to you and me," he admitted as he started to shuffle. "Adds a kind of dramatic symmetry to this whole affair, don't you think?"

Chad stared at him. He did not raise, nor even twitch, an eyebrow. Did not move save for the saliva that was dripping down from the top of his mouth in long globs.

"Are you a fan of symmetry, Chad?" he chuckled. He dealt all four cards with a few quick flicks of his wrist, watching them slide across the smooth purple felt of the table.

Chad lined his cards up one upon the other until the bottom one disappeared. He cast a discreet glance at the chips. He was slightly behind, but not by much. Not by as much as Brent seemed to think, which was just fine by him. Taking a deep breath, he bent back the corner of his cards, examined them for as little time as possible, then let them snap back to the table.

He did not answer the question.

Brent laughed, then pushed the deck to one side before checking his own hold cards. He smirked, took a sip of his drink, then leaned forward to stare at Chad again. "I am. A fan of it, that is. I like it when life works out into these sweet little fairytale moments that are so rare. I like it when the boy gets the girl, or the cop gets his man... or the hero faces off against the big bad poker shark."

Chad put out his blind, letting the chips scatter all over the space between them.

Brent did the same. "Make it eight thousand," he said, his mouth so large when he spoke that it showed off all the rounded off teeth in his head.

Behind him, Abby felt a sharp pain as her nails dug into her palm. It was only then that she realized how tight she'd been clenching them.

Chad watched him, watched every twitch on his grease covered face, then grabbed a stack of red chips and tossed them in. "Call."

Brent sneered, his nostrils flaring. He picked up the deck, burned one card, then started to deal out the remaining three. He clicked his tongue against the roof of his mouth. "First when I came to this city, I met this little fuck. This... what do they call them? This little person. A midget."

He flipped over the first card in line. It was a three of diamonds.

"He used to keep books for the big time crooks. Little fucker had a head for numbers like you wouldn't believe... guess when you can't wipe your own ass, you gotta make up for it with somethin'."

The next card turned, the seven of spades.

"Anyway, he really defied the stereotype. Didn't play into it at all, wouldn't put up with any bullshit. One guy four times his size called him a dwarf once, little guy had him layed him out cold on the floor five minutes later. Was quite a thing to see."

The third card. Nine of hearts.

"Five thousand," Chad said in a low voice, fighting to maintain eye contact despite the tale Brent was spinning.

"Ten," Brent chirped.

"Call."

He burned another card, careful to line it up precisely with the previous one just as Chad had his own a few moments ago.

"Had a normal wife, too. Got pissy if you called her normal, though. 'Average' was the correct term, he said. She was all politically correct, had no idea what he really did for a living. The crowd he hung around with. She was a knockout that didn't even see him as any different than her, even at the start. Rich too, from what he said. Trust fund back east or some such."

He flipped the turn card, its three red hearts glaring out at them both.

Abby took a breath.

Despite his best efforts, Chad reached down and bent up the corners of his cards again and let out the smallest of sighs.

Brent smiled.

"All in," Chad said, pushing his chips forward.

Brent stared at him a good long moment, then pushed all but two hundred dollars of his chips forward. He turned toward Abby and threw her a wink.

It made her feel sick.

He burnt one final card, then laid the river down at the end of the line, face down.

"Few months in, I find out he's been fucking around on her behind her back. Not an affair, though. Whores. Hookers. Different one every week, all ages and colours. Youngest was fourteen I think, but the oldest was damn near sixty. Man had a variety of tastes."

He reached out and tapped the river, but did not turn it. With every thud of his nail, Chad's eyes flicked from the card to his gaze and then back again.

"So I ask him one day: why? You've got a wife that doesn't care what a little circus freak you are who's hotter than hell itself. What the fuck are you doing spending your money on cheap ass hookers?"

"Is there a point to all this?" Chad asked finally, anger shadowing over his features. It was the first real emotion he'd let slip through since the hand began, and it decided to stay.

Brent smiled. "He told me: You have no idea how good it feels to fuck someone who thinks they're better than you.'"

He flipped the last card. It was the four of diamonds.

"I just wanted you to think about that, when you're flipping over your crappy hold cards there."

Chad stared at the four longingly for a moment, his eyes tearing up, then turned over his two. They were clubs, the king and jack.

"Ha!" Brent hollered, slapping over his. Three of clubs. Four of spades. Another full house. "Looks like your luck finally ran out, Matthews!"

Chad stared at the cards a moment, as Abby stepped up behind him and placed a shaking hand on his shoulder.

Brent raked the chips to his side of the table, even though the game was over. "Funny. Guess you're not so great at the cards anyway... I ended up ahead on this deal after all!"

The four diamonds glared at Chad, becoming a blurry line as his vision was cascaded by salt water.

"Come on," Brent smiled, knocking on the table to wake Chad from his trance. "I'll let you say goodbye before I take what you owe me out of her. I'm not a monster."

Chad's face turned red as he slowly turned up until their eyes met. His lips clamped tight, unspeaking.

"What do we do now?" whispered Abby.

CHAPTER 24

Salt Lake City, Utah

"She's in here," Cindy huffed, fiddling with the knob and cursing.

Victor watched from just over her left shoulder as the brass resisted her constant twisting, growing more and more impatient with each instant that passed. "Come on..."

"I'm going as fast as I can!" she hissed. "What do you care, anyway? Thought you were just another lowlife."

"I am," he drawled. "But that's rarely the whole story. Here."

He stepped between her and the door, lifting up on the knob. The door rose a half inch from the floor, and he gave it one hard push with his shoulder. It shoved forward, and he stumbled twice before getting his bearings against Brent's desk.

"There!" Cindy yelled, a smile spreading over her face as she ran over to the couch. Karen lay on it, still unconscious with a large welt on her forehead. But her petite breasts rose and fell with a slow, steady rhythm that brought immense joy to Cindy's heart. She hadn't realized how much she'd been worried until she felt the weight lift away. "Thank God you're okay!"

"No!" Victor yelled, slamming a fist down onto Brent's desk with enough force to crack it. "Not her, the girl! The *child*!"

"What child?" Cindy spat, turning to glare at Victor from over her shoulder. "What are you talking about?"

He ran his fingers through his long blonde hair, tugging hard at the roots. After a moment he slammed his fist down again.

Abby placed a hand against the knife in her pocket, pressing her finger alongside the handle to keep it straight as she followed Chad and Brent down the stairs. She could almost hear Diedre's fencing lessons replaying in her head as though she were speaking them now. Could imagine the marks on Brent's back as clearly as they'd been on the test dummy Diedre used to teach them where to jab. Where the arteries were.

Chad's face was streaming with tears now, but he forced his face taut. It leaked despite his best efforts at bravery, the fear and heartache bleeding through his facade like condensation finding its way out of a glass of water.

"Don't look so down," Brent said, approaching the doorway near the end of the hall and fishing a key out of his pocket. "Things could always be worse."

"Shut the fuck up," Chad barked, a bubble of mucus escaping from his right nostril. "You shut the fuck up right now. I'm gonna fucking kill you for this, you... you fuck."

Brent turned to him, a smile spreading over his lips. "You think that, do you?" he laughed a little, then turned his back to them both and slid the key in the lock.

Abby took the knife from her pocket and raised it high.

∞

Victor opened the back door to *The Pearl Necklace* with Cindy and Karen only a few steps behind, one propping up the other. The cool night air hit him as he spun around a full three hundred and sixty degrees, scanning the whole parking lot.

The only car there was his old El Dorado, which was vacant.

He ran his hands through his hair again, squatting down almost to the pavement and taking a deep breath.

"Where are they?" Karen asked, her words slurring together. "Where's Koy?"

CHAPTER 25

Salt Lake City, Utah

"Get up, girl. Time to say goodbye to your brother!" Brent laughed, swinging the door open wide just as Chad noticed Abby's blade and stepped out of the way.

Brent's eyes went wide, his mouth suddenly dry.

Abby brought down the dagger.

It slid back into her pocket harmlessly.

The room was empty.

There was no Koy, nor any sign that Koy had ever been there.

Brent turned back to Chad, furious. "You --"

Chad backed up a pace, his eyes wide and glossy. When Brent met them, he saw the same shock he felt immediately.

He looked from Chad to Abby and then back again, finally turning back toward the door. "Fuck!" he yelled, slamming his fist through the wall.

Abby smirked a little. "What do you suppose the chances of that were?"

Chad smiled.

"Eight... nine... five thousand," Victor finished, counting out the last of the money and planting it firmly into Sigmund's hand. "And my thanks."

"Keep it," he smiled, shovelling the cash into his breast pocket. "I can't spend thanks."

"Don't be so sure," Victor chuckled, turning to watch as Abby and Chad played with Koy while Karen watched from the couch. "A debt from me can go a long way. Don't be too eager to dismiss it."

Sigmund took a step toward Chad's front door, stopped, then turned back toward Victor. "How'd you know I'd get the kid? How'd you know I wouldn't just--"

"Take the money and run?"

"Like the song says," he smirked.

Victor regarded him with a long, heavy look for a moment, his features as blank as a statue. "Odds were someone like you would've had a price. A high price, but a price."

Sigmund paused a moment, his thick lips floundering from side to side, then nodded and stuck out his hand. "Pleasure doing business with you."

"The same," Victor said, pumping the man's arm firmly and then watching as he walked out the door. When the large figure disappeared from sight, he turned back toward the house and walked into the living room to join the others. "That was some stroke of luck we had there."

Chad laughed, snatching a blue elephant from Koy. She giggled playfully, tugging on Abby's shirt. "Was it? If I'd been lucky, I think maybe I would've won the game."

"Luck is subjective," Victor drawled, digging his

phone out of his pocket and flipping it to the text messaging screen. "It is what we make of it. By the time you lost, the kid was already out of that room. If you'd won, Joby would still be convinced you were his shot at fortune. He'd have kept coming."

"And now he won't?"

"If I did the math right on him."

"It certainly was on the dealer," Abby scoffed, rolling her eyes.

Chad paused, looking Victor up and down. "Certainly was."

Koy squealed happily, turning toward Victor's phone as it hummed to life.

CHAPTER 26

Los Angeles, California

Theo held his satchel close to him as he pushed through the crowd. The smell of sweat and smoke and road dust crowded his nostrils as the late afternoon sun beat down against his face. He ran his fingers through his pale blonde hair, matted and encrusted with dirt from days without showering, and let out a sigh.

Days like today were when it seemed like he would never find her.

It was useless using his eyes to scan the crowd for her face, he saw it everywhere now. Out of the corner of his eye he would see a flash of her auburn hair, or her brilliant green eyes twinkling mischievously. It would always be gone by the time he looked back, taunting him. Eyes were useless for this kind of thing. Instead, he turned to thoughts.

Closing his eyes he could scan a crowd of hundreds in seconds if all he paid attention to were the immediate thoughts, the ones currently on the forefront of their cerebellums. They stood out like billboards in the dark, spotlights shining up at them and displaying whatever the thought was in wonderful vibrant colour.

"He really thinks he can pass those off as real. Idiot."

"Dammit. At this rate, I'll never get to work on time. Bloody crowd."

"Little prick. Thinks I'd sell him a gram for that cheap."

The only problem with reading minds, he had found, was that there was no filter. You could get caught up in the tangle all of them at once, and in a venue as crowded as the marketplace, this could prove headache inducing.

He was looking for anything that would lead him to Abby, cursing himself that he didn't have more to go on. That he hadn't snatched more information from her and the man she'd left with nearly two weeks ago.

"Spilt milk," he huffed under his breath, noticing the thoughts of the few people close enough to hear him change briefly.

Weirdo.

Freak.

Dirtbag.

They went back about their normal trains soon enough, as did his. He reminded himself that it wasn't productive to think that way. He couldn't change the past, no matter how much he wanted to.

He cursed under his breath and started to scan the crowd again, their billboards lighting up his sky.

Pervert! One screamed in bright white letters against a black background, spotlights shining over it like the ones at a Hollywood premiere.

Another billboard moved, like an impossibly clear video was playing on it. There was a child on it crawling to her father for the first time, drool coming out of her mouth in copious bursts and she scrambled along the floor excitedly.

Beatles! A third billboard announced, and beneath it was a print of the *Sgt. Pepper's Lonely Hearts Club Band* album. He stayed on that one for a moment, and the music actually began to play as clearly as if it were over his own headphones.

"Got to admit it's getting better, getting better all the time..."

Theo opened his eyes and examined the three he'd just read. One was a middle aged woman that was glaring at a homeless man a few feet from her. Another was the father from the movie, leaned against the far wall and reading a newspaper. The third was a twenty-something girl that was dressed almost completely in hemp, sipping on Starbucks.

He frowned, then moved on. All he had to go on were names. Abby Fisher, Hunter Mason, and someone named Victor. That was it. Los Angeles was a big city, and the only reasons he had to be here were some thought fragments he had gotten from Hunter.

It had taken him a week to leave PHI, and then another two days to get to LA. By that time nine days had gone by, and they could have gone and left again.

"Fuck," he said. Winding toward a side street, he ducked out of the marketplace.

He had been 'people watching' there for two days, and was so focused on finding her he hadn't bothered to sleep or eat or even shower. He'd lived in this city for a while before discovering himself, and still had an apartment he owned there. He'd tried once or twice to sublet it while in PHI with less than desirable results, but now that seemed like one of the few blessings in this whole endeavor. Having a place to hang his hat, even briefly, had made this at least a little easier.

Shoving his hands into his pockets, he made his way toward the subway. The air was thick here compared to the forest he had become used to, something that made his despair seem tactile and environmental.

Chasing Abby had become like chasing invisible butterflies. He knew that she was somewhere near, that she was beautiful, that she was fragile, and that if he didn't find her soon someone else had the opportunity to catch her. He hated to think about it.

He moved toward the steps leading down to the subway.

A thick crowd had amassed around the steps, making his head throb. Every time he bumped against someone their thoughts intensified, to the point where it began to sound like yelling in his head. By the time he made it to the bottom of the stairs, his stomach had performed a backflip and he was nauseous, doubling over in the throes of a full-fledged migraine.

"Can I help you?"

Theo looked up to see an amused woman standing over him. Her raven hair was slicked back and almost conformed to the shape of her head. She wore a tight fitting army jacket and a long black skirt, her lips were painted into a little black pucker that reminded him of a gothic china doll.

He stared at her for a moment more before she spoke

again.

"Really, you don't look good. Do you need me to call someone for you?" She looked a little more worried now that he hadn't said anything.

"I'm fine. I was just feeling queasy. Something I ate, I'm sure," he lied, pressing a hand to his gut to try and sell his fabrication. "I've been on the move a lot, and I haven't had time for a decent meal really. Just fast food crap."

"Well, I hope you feel better soon," she said, looking a little relieved as she turned to leave. "There's nothing worse than being sick in this city."

"Thanks. Not many people would care to check on a stranger like that. Especially not here."

"I'm Leigh. Leigh Blackheart," she said, turning back toward him and smiling a little. "I'm the head of acquisitions for Shane International."

She held out her right hand to him, a slender black business card clasped between her middle and pointer fingers.

"Theo Flaherty. Artist," he responded reflexively as he took the card from her.

His fingers grazed against hers, and just like before his mind became awash with thoughts alien and yet familiar to him.

Darkness. Like ink, swirling on marble and glistening in the night. Bubbling beneath the surface, something raw and untapped... Slowly eating away...

Apartment 5A, 752 West 23rd street. Abigail and Hunter should be home soon. Victor might be with them, but I suppose that's a chance that I can afford to take.

Theo snapped back, the contact only having lasted

a millisecond of real time, but the thought process long enough to make him forget where he was, if only briefly. Instead of looking flabbergasted he remained composed, tucking the card into his pocket. "Well it was nice meeting you, Leigh. I'll see you around."

Leigh smiled. "I hope so, Theo. I really hope so."

She turned to leave, then glanced back over her shoulder, her large brown eyes twinkling at him.

There was something there that Theo couldn't quite place his finger on, but he hoped he'd be able to soon.

Now he had a location, though he wasn't sure how this new person fit into the mix.

He picked himself up gingerly, catching his reflection in the chromed finish of a pole as he did so. Gone was the blonde boy with sun kissed skin and blue eyes. In his place was a darkened man, hair held back with dirt, his blue eyes glaring fiercely. He was taken aback. He understood now why Leigh was one of the only people who had spoken to him since he left PHI. He looked like someone to be afraid of.

He made his way toward the terminal then, choosing a train that would lead him west and leaning against a post to wait for it.

CHAPTER 27

Los Angeles, California

Leigh ran a hand over the top of her head, breathing heavily. She had felt him going through her mind, and all she could do to stop him was give him what he wanted. She cursed. He had mesmerized her, and she had seen how much his power had caused him pain.

He knew my pain. she thought, bringing one of her sharp nails to her mouth and chewing it methodically.

She raised her hand into the air, hailing a cab. He would get there before her, she was certain. It would be better than him walking in on her though.

It seemed she had taken the perfect day off. Abby would be back in town, she could make her offer. Leigh smiled grimly. If anyone could help her, it would be Abby. No one else had near enough motivation or skill.

A yellow taxi pulled up beside her and she got in, ducking her head.

"752, West 23rd street," she commanded.

The driver glanced up at her in the rear view mirror and nodded.

She sunk back into the seat and relaxed. It would be a

long ride.

Smiling, she reached between her breasts and pulled out a slender key, running it between her fingertips in the gleaming light coming in through the cab windows.

"Should keep a better eye on your things, Theo," she smiled, its reflection caught in the blacks of her eyes. "It's a hell of a city."

Theo emerged from the subway station into a setting sun. Golds and reds and pinks clung to every building, reminding him of Abby and the painting he'd done of her. He wanted to know how Leigh knew them, if it wasn't just a coincidence. The woman was so unsettling in her beauty and strangeness, and had led him straight to Abby.

He stopped, clicking his tongue as facts finally clicked into place like the gears of a recently spun watch. He took out her business card and looked at it. Shane Industries was printed across the front in raised letters.

She worked for the same company that Abby had.

"You can't drive any faster than this? Really?" Leigh snapped, throwing her hands in the air.

"Hush, woman," the driver said, tossing an annoyed glance at the rearview mirror. "We're only half an hour away now. We're making good time for rush hour."

"Good time compared to what? Walking? God damn, I should've just taken the subway," she said, glaring. She stared at the glowing green numbers of the dashboard clock and huffed, running her nails over her scalp. She didn't want to think about what would happen if she missed her chance.

CHAPTER 28

Los Angeles, California

Theo reached Hunter's apartment building. It was the type of tall, gray building with small balconies that seemed to come with every large city in North America, as though they were part of some urban starter-kit.

He stood back away from the property, examining it with a critical eye that Port Haven had fostered over his time there. It was something he slid into naturally now, like a film student picking out the inconsistencies in a television show or an English major pointing out the grammar gaffs in a novella.

There were no balconies or ledges on the lowest floor, just largish windows with plastic guards on them that kept them from being opened fully. The fire escape going up the east side was in plain view of the street and was plastered with signs warning of video surveillance. Whether or not that was true was another story completely.

As he watched, a woman in her fifties made her way up to the main entrance. She pulled a key ring out of her petite purse but selected not a key, but a small blue plastic circle about the size of her thumb. She held it to a black pad between the two doors and it beeped audibly before a small light on it turned a bright green and she opened the door.

Theo squinted, nodded, then returned his attention to the street and waited.

A young man walked toward the main entrance, and Theo waited for him to pass as silently as he could, then ran to catch up.

"Hey, hold the door, kay?" he called out.

The man turned back, looking him up and down. There were dirt clods in his hair and he looked like he hadn't showered in days. "We're not supposed to let people in if we don't know them," he said passively.

"Yeah, I know," Theo smiled, laughing. "I'm staying with a friend. He just forgot to leave me his buzzer... I'm sorry man, if you could just help me out?"

He frowned. "I dunno..."

"Please?" Theo asked, reaching out and touching him on his bare forearm. Again a flood of images and memories not his own crashed into his consciousness like a tidal wave. He held on as long as he could, until he felt as though part of himself might get lost in the undertow.

The man flinched, and Theo released him. "Who are you staying with, anyway?"

Theo paused, mentally rummaging through the names and data he'd just gleaned.

Logan? Not the type to have guests.

Steve? Wouldn't have forgotten the key.

Jean? Jean.

"Jean," he said, after only a moment's pause. "I'm an

old friend of Jean's from college."

The man smiled. "Yeah, that sounds like Jean... alright. Hey, if you need keys or anything, the building manager lives in 1A. If you tell him the situation, I'm sure he'll let you in if no one comes to the door. We had some old lady die a couple of years ago, and no one found her body for weeks. He was pretty pissed that no one bothered to check on her, so now he plays pretty fast and loose with the keys."

Theo smiled at him. "Thanks. I'll definitely do that."

They both stepped in and Theo watched the man take the lead, walking directly for the elevators. He didn't pause to look back at the man he'd let in, or even wonder if the visitor was even headed in the right direction.

"The power of saying that right name," Theo said to himself, then turned toward the elevator and pressed the button for the fifth floor.

Reaching the top of the landing, he moved seamlessly toward the door to apartment 5A, pulling a beaten old leather wallet from his back pocket as he did so. From behind a soggy twenty dollar bill he produced a long, slender piece of metal and inserted it into the keyhole, twisted twice, then opened the door.

He closed the door behind him quietly. The apartment opened directly into the open concept kitchen and living room area. It was unremarkable, except for how immaculately clean it was. Every appliance was stainless steel, no dishes left on the counter or sink, and the dining nook was free of any crumbs or spills.

"Like walking into a goddamn show home," he said under his breath, sliding his pick back into his wallet.

He perused the living room, making sure not to leave anything out of place. He sat down on the couch, sliding open the drawer of the coffee table. The only items inside were a lighter and a package of tea light candles. He closed it again, feeling extremely dirty compared to Hunter. He was caked in dirt, going through the house of someone who was apparently hyper clean. He got up off the couch, then made his way toward the hall.

It was small and narrow, only three doors leading off of it. One lead to a bathroom, just as clean as the kitchen, with dark wood and black tile to match. A small glass held two toothbrushes and one tube of toothpaste. There was a single bar of soap that sat in a dish on the sink, and black hand towels hung on either side. Theo shuddered at how cold and un-lived in it felt.

The study lay across the hall from that. A dark wooden desk stood against one wall, the other wall hidden behind two tall bookshelves and a display case that held a collection of swords bigger than Theo's.

Something deep and masculine inside him hated that.

He moved toward the desk and opened a laptop that lay on top of it. It was in sleep mode, and when he shook the mouse, a box appeared on the screen.

RESTART SESSION?

Yes   No

CHAPTER 29

Los Angeles, California

Theo clicked the yes button and Hunter's e-mail came into view. The latest e-mail had come in only twenty minutes before, and was from Victor. It was still unread. He clicked on it, taking a deep breath.

Hunter,

Abby still doesn't know what her powers are. I want you to try and find out tonight. Maybe you'll be able to coax them out of her. Without them, I don't see why she's of much use to us, or why she's in danger. Are you sure you got the right girl?

That painting in your apartment, apparently her friend Theo painted it. It went missing the first night you were at Port Haven. Someone else was there besides you and the gang. Watch yourselves. Whoever it is knows where to find you, and is playing some kind of game with us. Not only that, my contact says that Theo left. He may be dangerous to you. Be careful.

-Victor

Theo looked at the screen, his lip curling up in disgust.

"Don't know who you are... but you have got to be the dumbest fuck I know if you've got the painting and still having figured out what she can do," he whispered to himself, then hit 'delete message' and closed the laptop screen.

There was only one room left where the painting could be. He got up, left the study and entered the bedroom.

The curtains were drawn to, and the first thing his eyes fell upon was a bouquet of roses resting on the bed, along with a note addressed to Abby.

Anger welled up inside him as he took in the rest of the room. Black sheets, a gold bed frame, and above that, the painting of Abby, looking for all the world beautiful and perfect. He made his way toward the bed, picked up the note, and read it.

Welcome home.

He snarled, ripped the note in two and snatched the bouquet off the bed. Furiously, he tore the heads off the roses and flung them to the ground, spinning around to search for something else to tear apart. His eyes landed on a large vase, which he gripped with white knuckled fingers and raised above his head. He flung it at the wall, the crimson pottery shattering and falling to the floor.

He glanced up at the painting again. Too perfect, too pleasant. Smiling even as tears of hate and loneliness and anger started to burn his way down his cheeks, he bent down, picked up a sharp shard of pottery and slit his wrist.

∞

Leigh slammed the door of the cab and threw her

money at the driver.

"Keep the change," she snarled. Brow creased, she stalked up to the front door of the building.

Glancing around to check if anyone was watching, she slid her hand toward the lock and let her finger gently slide in, liquefying and then hardening into shape. The green light blinked to life and made a mechanical droning sound as it shorted out. She turned the knob, pushed the door open and slid her finger out once again. Feeling it form back into place, she moved for the stairs.

Theo slumped to the floor, clutching his wrist and staring up at his handiwork. He chuckled to himself, coughed twice, then smiled and laughed again as he stared at this new portrait. "If she can't figure out her own power now…"

He didn't care anymore, he realized.

She hadn't returned his feelings. After months with him, she had barely gotten any closer to him, but after just two weeks with Hunter they'd all but moved in together.

His vision blurred. He shook his head, trying to see clearly. It didn't work and only succeeded in making him dizzy. Feeling his consciousness slip a bit, he descended closer to the floor and rested his face on the carpet.

Dimly, he was aware of a door opening and shutting, and of a single person entering the apartment.

"Abby?" he tried to say, though he couldn't hear anymore and wasn't sure if he actually had. His eyelids felt heavy, flickered, then closed.

CHAPTER 30

Los Angeles, California

Leigh glanced around the apartment. It looked sterile, but she could smell the pungent smell of dirt and blood. A sickening feeling settled in her gut, and she wondered again if she was too late.

She moved toward the hallway, and heard a voice mumble something. Only one door was open a crack, at the very end of the hall. She ran toward it, swinging it open fully.

Her eyes widened.

"Shit," she breathed, racing toward Theo.

He was hunched in a pool of blood, his eyes closed. Kneeling, she grabbed for his wrist, desperate to find a pulse. Instead, her fingers slid into a deep gouge. "Shit, shit, shit!"

She ripped a strip off her shirt, tying it quickly just above his wrist. She felt at his neck and waited for the faint 'ba-dump' of a pulse to let her know he was still there. One, two, three... She held her breath. One, two, three...

Finally it came, faint and unsteady. She picked him up

in her arms, staggering toward the door. "Have to get you out of here," she said to him, though she knew he couldn't hear her. "Back to your place, if I can. If I have the time."

He was still bleeding. She had to stop it. There had been so much blood. Too much blood… he couldn't die like this. She laid him back down on the floor and pressed her hand to the wound, letting her hand liquefy and close the cut. She could feel the blood pressing against her skin, trying to force its way out.

A black tear fell down her cheek as she tried to pick him up again, hand still pressed to his wound, as she tried to keep a steady pace.

∞

"I'm glad you met me here," Abby smiled, taking her luggage from the carousel.

"Like I said, I couldn't let you drive home alone this hour of the night," Hunter said, letting his hands slip around her waist.

She turned to face him, setting her luggage down beside her.

"How was Utah?" he snorted, raising a hand to brush one of her auburn curls from her cheek. "Learn much from Victor?"

"More *about* him, I think. I'll just be glad when we head back to Arizona. This whole escapade only proved there's safety in numbers."

"Then it's a good thing we'll be together tonight," Hunter said as he leaned in closer and placed a kiss on her lips. "Shall we hail a cab?"

CHAPTER 31

Northton, Idaho

Mary sat on the edge of the bed, holding the blanket tight to her naked body.

She shivered as the wind picked up outside, blowing in through the holes in the cobbled together shack. She quivered, sniffing loudly. Slowly she looked around the small, rundown little house.

The dark purple blanket she held to her was dirty and smelled like it had never been washed, filling her nose with the scent of old sweat and dead skin. There was a black splotch on it near her foot that looked sticky, though she wasn't going to touch it to find out. It might have once been gum that someone tried their best to get out, she thought. There was a spatter-like stain near where the bed met the wall, its edges white and flakey. The only one she recognized completely was a brown oblong next to her cheek that smelled like coffee.

The bed itself was wedged tight between three walls at the back of the cabin. They were made of varying colours and textures of plywood, birchwood and several panels that appeared to be fibreglass. It looked like someone had taken pieces from eight different jigsaw puzzles and then forced them together, despite the fact that they didn't fit. The result was varying. In some places the material was strong enough to keep out the wind, in others it was as effective as tissue paper. Animal skins had been tacked up in some places to try and solve this issue, at least on a provisional basis.

There was a thick layer of dust on the floor, clumping in the corners and under the bed to form dust bunnies. In some of these collections were tiny black flecks where silverfish had laid eggs, waiting to open and slither out along the floorboards.

There was a black cast-iron potbelly stove a few feet from the foot of the bed, the fire crackling and snapping at her through its grate. It was roaring beautifully, but did very little to stop the cold. A twisting pipe that looked like something out of a Tim Burton film ran from the stove and up to the ceiling, churning out barrels of black curling smoke.

There was a small cooler not far past the stove, against the far wall. She didn't think it would keep much cool. Also against the far wall was a large metal chest that looked like it was two centuries old. The rusted padlock on the front of it hung open and she didn't think the hinge would move if she tried with all her strength.

On the opposite side of the room from the chest was a large homemade workbench and chair. There were knives stuck into the wood, some rusted and some clean. The table's airy surface was covered in blood, almost painted in it. A long, serrated knife sat in the center of the goopy, congealing pool, covered in redness itself. There was a spool of barbed wire twisted into spirals near it, several tiny specks of flesh hanging from its hooks.

She shivered again and felt like she might vomit, yet could not look away now that she'd seen it. The entire building was less than ten feet squared, so there was no place for her to go to escape the sight or the scent which she was now sure she could smell above even the fire or the blanket or the dead animals hanging from the wall.

There was a scuttling, dragging sound outside. She gasped and yelped, holding the blanket tight to her face despite its vulgarity and stared at the door with those massive blueish-green eyes.

The sound continued now, closer and closer until it was actually coming from the side of the shack, some force dragging something across its siding. It stopped suddenly, and there was a long moment where even the wind seemed to hold its breath.

Then the door flew open, seemingly of its own accord, revealing the man that stood there. He was breathing hard, his chest rising and falling in great heaves. Even though his yellowed eyes had no pupils, she knew he was staring right at her.

He was thin... almost emaciated, as though there weren't enough skin to cover his body, making it stretch out and become slightly translucent and pale. He was naked from the waist up, his ribs clearly visible. A flap of skin under each set shook back and forth with every breath he took.

His muscles were lean, his arms and legs both too thin and long for the size of him, making him look like the human equivalent of a daddy longlegs. His bones bulged at the joints, creaking and crackling with even the slightest movement.

His palms were large and plump, as were his fingers. There were only two per hand and a thumb that sprang from the center of the palm rather than the side. They were dirty and his fingers were covered in hot, sticky redness. His nails were yellowed and thick, looking like small plates of wood on the tips on his fingers rather than parts of his anatomy.

His feet were long... if he'd been wearing shoes, they would have had to have been at least a size seventeen. They were thin like the rest of him, their bones creasing as he wriggled his toes, of which there were only two. They appeared to have joints, like fingers. A third toe protruded out the back of his foot, its nail chipped and worn.

His body was hairless, the chest muscles large and full and making him look uneven. His head was too large as well, appearing as an oval that came down to a point at his chin. He was naturally bald with no discernable earlobes, just a lumpy mound of skin around duel holes where they should have been. His eye sockets were too large for his eyes, leaving pinkish muscle around the rims and making him appear sinister. His hairless brow curled down at her, making them take on a triangular shape.

There was no nose, just two thin triangular nostrils that travelled right up to his sinuses.

His mouth looked too big for his face, and was filled with sharp, gray teeth.

Mary gasped when she saw them, dropping the blanket.

He smiled.

CHAPTER 32

Los Angeles, California

"Jesus, my head..." Theo breathed, his eyes flickering open. His temples pounded to the beat of some exotic drum, a bright light from above entering through his corneas and becoming a million little razors. He shut them quickly.

The air was thick with the pungent stench of antiseptic, and he felt the pull of thread sliding through the taut skin of his wrist. He tried to open his eyes again, squinting toward the source of the odd sensation.

He jolted when he realized he was lying on his own bed, strapped down to the bedframe by old belts and cloth bedding. He was wearing only his pants, his naked chest heaving as anxiety and claustrophobia quickly crept their way in and stole his breath.

Leigh was kneeling by the edge on the bed, his wrist cradled in her hand, suturing the deep gouge he'd made in it shut. She was wearing a plain black bra and the same skirt as before.

"Why are we both topless?" he slurred.

Leigh glanced up, her pale face drawn and frightened. "You bled all over my jacket, and I used my shirt to make you a tourniquet," she whispered.

She bowed her head again and continued stitching him up.

He watched her between the black spots forming in his vision, then suddenly felt nauseous. "Did you drug me?" he mumbled, shutting his eyes again to keep the pain at bay.

"Just Ibuprofen. The rest of what you're feeling is from losing so much blood." Her voice was still hushed, and he felt her draw the last piece of skin together. She paused for a moment and all he could hear was her breathing.

He let out a deep sigh and tried to raise his free hand to rub the bridge of his nose, only to be reminded immediately that it was restrained.

"Why did you do it?" she whispered, and Theo felt her slight weight move as she lifted off the mattress.

"I don't know," he frowned, scrunching his face together.

She sighed and left the room without another word.

He laid his head back onto a pillow he hadn't felt in ages, yet still seemed to retain the shape of his scalp. Closing his eyes, he let a tingling, gentle sensation wash over him until he forgot where he was or how he'd gotten there, unsure of how long she was gone and not caring.

She returned minutes later and sat back on the bed. She lifted his wrist up, and he felt her slip a strip of gauze under it, roll it around, and create a layer of bandage. She was silent again, the rhythm of her breathing slightly shallow.

"Are you okay?" he asked.

She stopped wrapping. "Just a bit sick myself. It takes a lot of energy to keep myself together, I guess," Leigh whispered, forcing the bandage closed with a clasp. "You should be fine soon though. Just don't pull another stunt like that, okay? You never know who might need you…" She got up again.

"Leigh, wait." The sentence came out as a desperate plea.

"I won't go yet. Don't worry," she said, still sounding frightened.

"Thank you," he whispered.

He passed out again.

Hunter pushed open the apartment door and backed in, smiling. He held the door for Abby, not letting her out of his sight.

"There's a surprise for you in the bedroom." He smiled devilishly, the way he had when they'd first met.

She looked past him and into the apartment. "Oh my god."

All she could see was the blood. Her fingers loosened and her bags dropped to the floor with two solid thuds.

Hunter turned around and the smile fell from his mouth and became something different, a scowl so vicious that it almost looked alien on his sweet face. "What the hell…" he growled.

Her hands cupped against her mouth as he started through the apartment, bracing himself against the archway that led into the hall for a moment before disappearing past it.

All she could see was the blood.

Hunter's apartment had been as clean and as sterile as a surgeon's table, all whites and blacks and smooth, shimmering silvers. Now there was red everywhere, staining everything in splotches and spatters that defiled the very nature of it. As though someone had gone out of their way to take everything she'd loved about this place and slash at it with redness, exposing it as the lie it was.

"Abby, come in here!" Hunter yelled from the bedroom.

She followed him down the hallway to where he stood at the bedroom door, her feet daintily following the hodge-podge trail of blood that had strewn its way along the floor.

"Abby, the painting…" he sighed, looking at her with some mix of horror and subdued rage.

She moved into the room, dodging the large pool of blood that was seeping into the carpet. Above the bed was the painting Theo had done of her. It was covered in streaks of drying blood, still beautiful but also haunting. Rather than a woman exploding in fire, she now looked possessed, eyes hollows of red with droplets of blood springing forth.

She looked like an angel of death.

"Theo…" Abby whispered, moving closer to the painting. She barely took in the crumpled roses she walked over, even as their thorns pierced the arch of her foot.

She turned to Hunter. "Get Victor here."

CHAPTER 33

Los Angeles, California

Leigh slid open Theo's closet door.

She brushed her hands along the row of shirts that hung neatly, glancing over her shoulder to where he lay on the bed before extracting a gray dress shirt, a white tee shirt, and a pair of clean pants from the closet. She laid the dress shirt and the pants on the bed, sliding the white tee shirt on over her head.

She had taken the restraints off Theo, and he lay there peacefully now with the belts limp and useless on either side of him. He was still covered in grime, and she debated whether or not to drag him out to the tub or leave him.

Letting out a sigh she moved toward him, slipped one arm beneath him and lifted. Grunting once as they started to move, she made her way toward the bathroom with his head cradled against her chest.

Slipping him into the tub, she removed his pants and propped his head and arm against the rim. She paused, tapping the arch of her forefinger against her black lip and wondering if she should remove his underwear. Recalling how he'd reacted to their being shirtless, she thought better of it and started the water.

Glancing around for the soap, she finally found a bottle on a shelf above the toilet. Removing the cap, she squirted some onto a cloth and turned off the water.

Kneeling down by the side of the tub, she began to gently massage the dirt off of Theo's chest. His face was relaxed looking, the painkillers slowly working their magic. She allowed herself a small smile as she moved to wash his hair, gently holding his head in her palm.

She squeezed the cloth over him and a small amount of water trickled over his scalp, wetting his hair before she lathered the soap into it. He stirred slightly and she slowed her hand, watching as he began to mumble his way back to consciousness.

His eyes flickered open.

"What are you doing?" he mumbled.

"Cleaning you up," she said, laughing at how confused he looked. "You stink."

"Don't you have anywhere to be?"

"You made that place a little bloody. I figured I'd let it die down there first, and try back another time." She smiled shyly at him. "Besides, who else would be fixing you up?"

He returned the smile, eyes closing of his own accord and relaxed into her touch. "You saved my life."

She laughed again. "You state the obvious."

Leigh rinsed the cloth in the bath water, then brought it back to pour more over his hair. The soap rinsed down over his face and into his eyes, but he didn't respond to it.

She moved him forward slightly in the tub so she could wash his back, squirting a tiny bit more soap onto the cloth. She was at an odd angle, twisting to reach him.

"You know, it'd be easier if you were in the tub behind me," Theo said, eyes still closed. Leigh paused.

"Wouldn't that be weird though?" she asked slowly.

"No, it would be easier. It's not like you've harmed me, you've only helped. I might as well make it easier on you." He turned his head to face her, and now she could see a stillness in his eyes. It was odd to see, a man without intent or agenda or even hope. At least for the moment, he just... was.

"Thank you?"

She got up and pulled the tee shirt off, then her skirt. She slid into the tub behind Theo, the cool air of the bathroom replaced by the heat of the water almost instantly. She knelt behind him and continued to wash his back, the soapsuds traveling down it and clinging to her skin.

"So why were you going to see Abby?" Theo asked her.

Leigh stopped scrubbing.

"It's personal, really. She used to work at the same place I do now. I had some questions for her about why she left... It's for another time now though."

Theo turned to face her, studying her face carefully. She felt him try to pry into her mind and fail. "Why can't I tell what you're thinking now?" he whispered.

"You're probably still too weak," she blushed. "That much blood loss requires a bit of time to recover."

He was looking straight at her, still trying to read her and suddenly making her feel very naked.

"You're all clean now. Make sure not to get your arm

wet, okay?"

She lifted herself up from the tub a tiny bit, but his good arm caught hers, pulling her back down. Her breath got caught in her throat as she fell awkwardly back into the water with a small splash.

"Why did you stop to help me?" Theo breathed, brushing hair back from her ear as he leant in to kiss her neck.

"I know what it's like to feel that kind of pain. To know it's not safe to spend the night in the same place twice." Her breath was shallow as she felt Theo's lips brush along her earlobe. He held her arm still, and cradled her cheek with his other hand. She could sense her body quivering as he held her, but did not pull away.

His dried, pink lips caught her small black ones, and he proceeded to pull her in. He cupped her thigh with his good hand, bringing the other down from her cheek clumsily to undo her bra. She made a small choking noise, but kissed him back harder before pulling away and gasping for air.

"I thought you came here looking for Abby. What made her so worth dying for?"

"Nothing. She's not worth anything to me anymore." His clear blue eyes looked deep into hers as he leant in to plant another kiss on her lips.

"I won't be anyone's second choice."

"I think I'm hoping for a little something more," he said, then brought the hand resting on her thigh in closer to her body, sliding it down her thigh and to her ankles.

Her big, black, doe eyes never left his, and it took her a moment to realize she was naked.

"You don't have a problem with that, do you?" he asked her, resting his forehead against hers and bringing her body closer to his.

She shook her head, fumbling fingers reaching into the shallow water toward him.

"You think Theo did all of this?" Victor asked, kneeling in the center of Hunter's apartment with one hand touching the floor. He picked up a battered copy of *To Kill a Mockingbird* that had been spattered heavily and examined it before laying it back down.

"The painting gives a pretty clear picture, if you'll pardon the pun." Hunter scoffed from his place standing next to the kitchen table. Abby was sitting at it, and he had one hand rested on her shoulder.

"He'd be a corpse on the front lawn unless someone else was here, too," he mulled, not really to either of them but to himself. He brought his hand to his mouth and drummed his thumbnail across the ridges of his teeth the way ex-smokers did for a moment before turning back and locking eyes with Abby. "Is there anyone else from Port Haven that might have come out with him?"

"No," she said quickly, then paused to think before speaking again. "No. I mean, we aren't really supposed to just up and leave. Actually, I think Theo's the only person from PHI that even had a place to stay outside of the grounds."

"He had an apartment in the city?" Hunter asked, raising an eyebrow.

"Since before he enrolled. Long before, from what I hear. He had bought it."

"There's at least another person," Victor interrupted, making no effort to hide his impatience. He locked eyes with Hunter. "He lost too much blood to have left here alone. You can't tell that?"

He stood up and started pacing back and forth through the blood filled apartment. The phone in his breast pocket hummed and he brought a hand to it quickly, silencing it without looking at the message.

"You think I chose to come home and find fucking blood everywhere?" Hunter retorted, throwing his arms up in the air.

"Can the two of you just shut the fuck up with the sniping please?" Abby huffed, her redheaded fury returning. "My friend was obviously here, *someone* obviously lost a lot of blood, and we kind of need answers!"

"I'm more worried about how the hell they found out where I live, Abby," Hunter droned. "There are worse things that could have happened. We could have been here. You could have been here."

"Break it up," Victor commanded, his voice firm and authoritative. "We're going to have to deal with people knowing where you live for now, Hunter. That's the price you pay for freedom. You don't get the security of numbers."

Hunter looked as though he wanted to speak, but did not.

"But we do need answers," he sighed, turning to Abby. "You're both going to have to wait here for the night though, until I can track down Theo. God forbid you have an actual emergency while I'm gone, the way you're acting."

Abby and Hunter looked at each other in silence.

When Victor was sure neither one had any retort, he turned and left without a sound.

CHAPTER 34

Los Angeles, California

Leigh awoke naked in a tangle of sheets. Her skin was a peculiar ashen colour she had only ever achieved before after two full minutes without oxygen, and she shuddered to think why that would be.

Theo lay beside her, chest rising and falling peacefully. He looked like an angel, curled so perfectly in the sheets that all she wanted to do was stay and bask in his warmth. She couldn't ever remember feeling this happy, and any negative thoughts were immediately pushed away. She leant down and, brushing away his bangs, planted a kiss on his forehead before leaving.

A piercing pain splintered through Theo's arm as he rolled over, falling off the bed and landing in a heap. He cursed, trying to extract his bad arm from the tangle of sheets he'd awoken into.

His hair was matted to the nape of his neck, a mass of blonde knotted and tangled with sweat. He laid back in the sheets, exhausted just from trying to get up. He had no idea how he and Leigh had… well, even the thought of that was a little exhausting.

Theo sat bolt upright. Where was she? None of the times when he had fluttered between consciousness and unconsciousness had she left, but now she was nowhere to be seen. He felt an ache form in the center of his chest and immediately begin to grow, and he spread his mind out through the apartment to sense for her sweet presence.

Nothing.

Sighing, he pulled himself up, using the mattress to brace himself. He dangled his feet over the edge and touched them to the floor tentatively. When he found he wasn't too unsteady on his feet, he made his way to the bathroom.

He leaned against the rim of the sink and splashed cold water against his face. His eyes caught their reflection in the mirror, bloodshot with the scruffy beginnings of a full-fledged beard. He opened the medicine cabinet and removed his razor and shaving cream, laying them against the sink with a sharp clack of porcelain.

Squirting some of the foamy cream into his palm, he brought his hands to his face and began to create a healthy lather over his cheeks and neck. He breathed in, slipping his hands back under the flow of tap water to rinse them free of residue. Trying to clear his mind, he lifted the razor to his cheek and slid it down toward his neck. He exhaled slowly, tapping the razor against the sink to release the stubble and foam before beginning the process anew.

Tony Chavez crushed the butt of his cigarette under the heel of his boot, letting the last dregs of smoke pass between his lips. He let his hand dance over his scalp, pushing back loose hair so it would stick into place.

Across the street, lights flickered in a warehouse, and he could see the outline of men fighting. Let them get it out now, he thought. It was just as well that they had their differences resolved before they had to work.

He snorted, then smiled. If a few of them took each other out, it would mean less of a split on the take.

CHAPTER 35

Los Angeles, California

Leigh sat at the edge of the overpass, choking on tears. She couldn't stop shaking, hands and lips a dark blue. Black smudges ran down her cheeks, making her look wild eyed as she stared at the cars speeding below her. A small sob escaped her and, doubling over, she retched onto her side. A small splash of bile hit the concrete, and she felt another shudder go through her small body.

"Fuck," she moaned.

The wind blew an uncharacteristically chilly breeze as stars filled the sky. She wore nothing but the thin shirt she'd stolen from his closet and her skirt, the wind whipping at her as if she were nothing more than a moth in a gale. She clutched at her arms, a dark smudge pulling at her.

She grabbed at the railing behind her, still trembling as she pulled herself in. She coughed again, more bile hitting the pavement as she struggled to walk toward the lights of a diner.

Stumbling inside, she clutched the door for support,

vaguely recalling having been at the same diner some years before. The room was blurry now, and she couldn't tell for sure.

Behind her, she heard a man yell.

"Bathrooms for paying customers only!" the cook shouted, trying to make himself heard over the spitting of the grill. "I don't need any addicts O.Ding in there."

She shut her eyes and kept walking, the cook returning to the orders of his patrons.

Pushing open the door to the female restroom, she collapsed to the floor and reached up to lock the door behind her. Her fingers fumbled with the knob clumsily, and when she was at last sure the door was secured she let her arm fall back to her side with a thud.

She tried to pull herself up, crawling toward the toilet before heaving into it. Under the fluorescent lights, it was clear what colour her bile was. It was inky black.

She heaved again.

CHAPTER 36

Los Angeles, California

Theo brought the fluffy white towel to his cheek, drying his face, then let it fall to the floor and flicked the bathroom lights off. He felt refreshed, as he always did when he was clean shaven.

He smiled a little to himself.

The only thing that could have made it better would have been if she had stayed. He had her number after all, or at least her business number. He wouldn't let her go that easily.

He made his way toward the kitchen, freshly bandaged and wearing black jeans. Not a speck of blood was visible anywhere in his apartment. He had no idea how Leigh had managed to get him in without making a mess, but he was glad she did. There was nothing like scrubbing to make someone feel dirty again.

Opening a cupboard, he slid out a tall glass and almost dropped it with his damaged arm. The bandages stared back at him and reminded him of what he'd done, what he'd tried to do, but it seemed like a lifetime ago now. A very long, stupid lifetime.

He brought the glass toward the sink and filled it with water, then raised it toward his lips and took a long drink, downing half the glass before a loud knock came on the door.

He froze, gasping for air after the long mouthful. He stared at the door and waited for the second knock to come before he set the glass down quietly in the sink and walked toward his display case. He selected a katana.

His eyes flicked toward the door and he let his mind stretch out, surprised when it hit a hard block. Moving slowly toward the door, he reached out and swung it open.

Victor stood in the archway, not flinching even at the sight of the blade in Theo's hand. His eyes were locked tight onto the younger man's, as though he'd known exactly where he was going to be standing right down to the tilt of his head. "I'm not here to hurt you, Theo."

Theo let his hand fall away from the door, and felt the katana fall harmlessly to his side. "What do you want then?" he spat.

He shook his head and massaged his temples with his forefingers. "My name's Victor."

"That doesn't sound like any kind of an answer," Theo snarled.

Victor sighed. "I'm a friend of Abby's."

Theo squinted, then tried to read him again. Tried so hard that the back of his own head itched, then finally gave up. Frowning, he laid the katana against the wall and stepped back inside, motioning for Victor to follow with a nod of his head.

The taller man obliged, stepping in and looking around the apartment as Theo found his way to a chair.

"Is she alright?" he asked finally, running his hands through his hair.

"Funny, that's pretty much what she asked of you."

Theo snorted. "Somehow I doubt that."

"You want to stop acting like the whole world is out to hurt you," he said, folding his arms in front of him. "Once you come to grips with that, you might be able to set yourself to being a half decent human being."

"What would you know about it?"

Victor gestured toward the stitches keeping Theo's arm together. "More than you'd think. More than I'd like to admit."

He rolled his eyes and frowned.

"You planning on heading back to Port Haven?"

"Not much point, now," he said glumly. "I don't think it'll ever feel like home again. Not after today. Not after knowing what home really feels like."

Victor squinted at him, clicking his tongue back and forth inside his mouth. "Get your ass in gear, then. Pack some stuff, because safety in numbers doesn't do you much good here alone."

Theo made eye contact with him again, and didn't know whether to laugh or to cry. "What makes you think I'll come with you?"

He did not respond, save for raising one of his bushy eyebrows as high as it would go.

After a moment in silence, Theo walked back into the bedroom he and Leigh had shared a few hours ago and started to pack a bag.

Abby pulled her hair back from her face as she bent down to rub more bleach over the floor. Her nose wrinkled in disgust as she plunged the red soaked cloth into the bucket of murky cleaning fluid. Not only did she hate the smell of blood, but the smell of pine cleaner made her stomach turn.

"Fucking hell. He really had to slice himself up, didn't he?" Hunter grumbled, pushing broken shards of pottery onto a dustpan. "We might as well start hunting for a new apartment, all the fucking blood here."

"I don't know if you've listened to anything Victor said, but we clearly can't stay here for long anyway," she said, shooting him a sideways glance. "Just for tonight, then we're all on the next plane to Arizona."

"Well I don't know if you've noticed, Miss Fisher, but I don't exactly follow Victor around like a little lost puppy," he said, not meeting her eyes. "I survived in this city before I met him, and I'll survive here when the rest of you are gone."

"What's that supposed to mean?" She stopped scrubbing the floor to stare at him, laying down the cloth and making another small puddle of dark red water when it hit.

"I'm not going to Arizona," he said in a dismissive, condescending voice. "It's not my scene."

"'Not your scene'? I really don't like it when you talk like this. You sound like a douchebag."

"I was going to offer you the opportunity to stay here with me tonight, but then all of this... Victor and I just don't get along well."

"So you just expected me to go along with you, when the whole time you've been telling me we needed to have Victor's protection?" Abby looked at him incredulously. "Jesus Christ, do you realize how fucking annoying it is to be yanked around like this? I can at least tell Victor's level headed. You on the other hand… I have no fucking clue."

"So you're saying all the times I've saved your neck mean nothing now? All the times I've been there for you? Whatever." Hunter got up and stormed out of the room. "I'm fucking through."

He slammed the door behind him.

"You really aren't anything like Jasper, are you?" Abby whispered, to no one but herself.

CHAPTER 37

Los Angeles, California

Theo scooped up the last of his carefully wrapped blades and pushed them into a large duffel bag. Victor stood over him, holding a larger bag filled with Theo's clothes and toiletries. "That's about the last of it."

"You got any family who're gonna miss you?" Victor watched him, eyes calculating as Theo got up.

"None. It's only my father and me left, and he thinks I'm still at a Black Springs. He wouldn't miss me anyway." Theo's eyes flashed, as if daring Victor to ask more.

"Black Springs?"

"Mental Facility."

"What were you there for?" His voice was inquisitive, and slightly amused.

"When you hear voices, people generally do assume you're crazy," Theo spat.

"So I'm guessing Port Haven pulled you out because you're telepathic, and not schizophrenic?" Victor said, smirking a little out the corner of his mouth.

Theo turned to him, squinting. "How'd you know?"

"You don't think you're the only person around like you, do you?" he grinned, turning to leave.

She couldn't breathe.

She had given up trying to fight the retching hours ago, or so it seemed. Everything felt like an eternity when she was like this.

Leigh could feel the blood in her veins chugging along sluggishly. She was lightheaded, trying to fight against the change and for oxygen simultaneously. Her vision remained blurred, but what she could see of her skin was almost entirely a terrifying tint of blue. She couldn't last like this for much longer.

She knew what would come. The frightening collapse of her lungs, the feeling of all of her organs melding together, squeezing any oxygen left in her body out, then the dizzying feeling as she passed out. The fear that would come with not knowing when or even if she would wake up. For the life of her, she had no idea how she had survived any of the other times. She would always come back though, perfectly whole and solid, just as the tinge of blue-black ink left her skin. Always, the voice at the back of her mind screaming, *This has to be the last time. What could be worse than this?*, and then the next time would bring her inches closer to death.

It was coming closer. Her vision began to go black, and she closed her eyes. Breathlessly, she made one last silent prayer, conjuring Theo's face into her mind before she passed out.

∞

The buzzer sounded in Hunter's apartment.

Abby looked up from where she scrubbed the floor, her hair a sweat laden mess. The tiny white box on the wall stared back at her with its single blinking red light, apparently the only item in the entire living room that had been spared Theo's bloodshed.

Huffing in exhaustion, she walked over and pressed the intercom button.

"Hurry up you two. I've got Theo here now, and the boy doesn't pack light," came Victor's gruff voice.

Abby smiled. "Okay, hurry up yourself. I need extra hands cleaning." She let her finger fall from the button, sighing in relief. He was alive. She allowed that to sit with her for a moment, before turning back and calling into the hallway. "Hunter, do you have any of the other rooms clean yet?"

"Study's done. Bathroom has seen better days, but I'm sure he can plunk his bloody ass down with no problem," Hunter snarled, rounding the corner and entering the living room. "Where are you sleeping?"

She was taken aback, still not used to his brutishness. "I'll take the study, I guess. Pull out a few blankets over the floor or something... Are you going to be ok?"

"I'll manage."

Victor's loud knock cut off any more of the conversation. Abby exhaled softly, walking toward the door and opening it.

"Take this one," Victor grunted, thrusting the larger duffel bag he had been carrying at Hunter, who had slunk up behind Abby.

"I've just finished explaining to Abby that I'm not

your slave," he spat, dumping the bag in the middle of the living room. "So stop treating me like one."

Victor shot Abby a stern look from beneath the hairs that looped down in front of his face. "I suppose you've gotten acquainted with his less pleasant side?"

"All goddamn day," Abby said, rolling her eyes. "I can't wait to get away from him."

"I take it he told you he wasn't coming? Don't get too upset either way. He has to go back to Tasha at some point," Victor smirked.

"Tasha?" Abby asked.

Victor waved a hand, shaking his head. "Old friend. Not important, not right now anyway."

"Oh... Where's Theo?" Abby looked around the hulking man, noticing for the first time Theo was not present.

"Right here," Theo called out, grunting from the stairs as he heaved the last bag up. "The landlord was wondering what was going on. Had to let him know that everything was okay."

Abby pushed past Victor and looked like she was about to give Theo a hug. He stepped back a pace and she stopped, the both of them regarding each other strangely for a moment.

"Let me get it for you," she smiled, breaking the tension between them. "You should be resting."

"I got it," he drawled, brushing past her and striding into the apartment. He threw his duffel bag down next to the first. He stopped and looked around the apartment. It was no longer immaculate, but it was nowhere near as dirty as he'd been expecting. "Cleaned up nice."

"About that...?" Abby asked, timidly.

"Meh. I was stupid. Wasn't thinking straight," he shrugged. "Helped me get my priorities sorted out, at least."

She narrowed her eyes at him, her cheeks becoming red with anger.

Victor sighed, stepping off to one side.

"You did this yourself?" she spat, taking one accusatory step forward. "You were trying to kill yourself?"

Theo frowned. "I don't know what I was trying to do."

"Well, there's only so many things slitting your fucking wrists will accomplish," she barked, grabbing his bandaged arm and holding it up, as if to show it to him. "You weren't trying to bake brownies."

"I was trying to give you a hint, okay Miss Priss? Stop your whining," Theo shot back. "Just let me be, okay?"

Abby nodded slowly. "One question though…"

"What?" Theo snarled.

"A hint for what?"

He opened his mouth to speak, then stopped and sighed.

From the kitchen, Victor watched and stroked his scruff methodically.

CHAPTER 38

Los Angeles, California

The sky was starting to fade to morning by the time Abby and Hunter had trailed off to bed. Neither of them had spoken, and Theo took slight pleasure in noting that they had both gone into separate rooms.

It was quiet in the living room when Theo removed his socks and shirt and plucked at the gauze on his arm. It looked worse, perhaps, in the dim light of dawn. He grimaced.

Street noise filtered in through the screen door of the patio, and he began to walk toward the door. He slid it open, breathing deeply as the new air of morning hit his face. Something about Los Angeles always woke him up, even when he hadn't had any sleep.

Yellows and blues mixed with hazy smog, drifting softly over the rooftops of office buildings and apartments and casting the city in a soft golden glow. No other time of day could make a place that was so hard become something so beautiful. As soon as the sun rose fully, as it was bound to do, this glamour would be gone.

He cussed softly, brushing a sleepy hand across his brow. He didn't want to have to leave it all behind again. He had only just gotten it back.

Gentle footsteps pattered behind him, and as he turned, Theo was surprised to come face to face with Hunter.

They stared at each other for a moment, looking each other up and down like two gunslingers squaring off on some dusty road.

"Can I help you?" Theo said finally, tapping his trim nails against the guardrail.

"Not really. I've just been thinking…" Hunter trailed off.

"Yeah? How's that working for you?"

"Not the greatest actually," he chuckled quietly.

"And what do you expect telling me to do?"

"I don't need any more enemies. Abby's all fucked up in the head, Victor hates my guts… I don't need to be at war with you, too." He extracted a thin cigarette and a pack of matches from his pants pocket. He lit it and inhaled deeply before continuing. "I need allies, you know? People to call my own. There's enough shit going on, more than Victor's letting on… I can't go back with Tash, she's got enough on her plate without me."

"So, what? You expect me to just be buddy buddy with you now that we're not fighting for Abby's attention?"

"Sure. Whatever floats your boat, dude," Hunter shrugged, blowing a ring of smoke into the morning.

Theo found his eyes glued to the apparition, following it until it became nothingness. "Well, I don't have any problem with that," he said, waving his hand through his hair.

"You want a smoke, man?" Hunter asked, offering Theo the pack.

"Naw, it's cool. I don't need that shit," he laughed, leaning against the rail. His eyes turned toward the horizon again.

There was loud knock on the door, shattering their amicability.

"Victor back again?" Hunter asked, tossing a glance at Theo as he snuffed his cigarette on the rail and flicking it down onto the street.

"Dunno. Can't read him."

"Let's go check it out."

They reentered the living room. Theo slid the screen door shut and Hunter walked ahead. Just as they reached the hall, Abby appeared in the darkness of the hallway.

"What's going on? Who's at the door?" she said, a tired doe-eyed expression on her face as she attempted to flatten her hair.

Hunter shrugged, reaching down into Theo's duffle bag and taking one of the swords out. He handed it back to Theo without looking.

Theo took it as quietly as possible and Hunter's hand went down again, his gaze never leaving the door the whole time.

Abby's expression was puzzled, watching these two men creep about in the darkness as though they were a part of it.

Hunter went for the peephole of the door. "No one there," he said finally. "Must have had the wrong apartment."

He backed away from the door and walked toward

the bag, bending over to lay the sword back down.

The door burst in and slammed him in the rear, sending him sprawling onto the dufflebag.

"Get that bitch!" Tony yelled, thrusting a finger toward Abby.

Four men clattered into the apartment, their clothes so black that they were nearly invisible.

Theo braced himself with the sword as one plowed into him before he had time to react. As the man collided with him, his forearm came up and slammed into the intruder's neck. The man fell, coughing as he suffocated on his own blood.

Hunter found himself with a foot against the back of his throat, his own blade inches from his fingertips. Eyes wide with fear, he stretched his hand toward the handle, hoping to grasp it. The man let his foot sink heavier.

Pushing the gasping man off of him, Theo sprung toward Hunter grasping his katana tightly and bringing its handle forward into the thug's eyes. The man pulled off of Hunter and screamed as blood squirt from either side of the impact, reeling away from the flash of silver as it came around to strike him. Theo managed to graze his cheek as Hunter pulled up, retrieving his sword and driving it into the thug's chest.

A shriek broke through the action as a vase crashed behind the boys. They turned simultaneously, Theo letting out a cry as they raced toward two men pulling at Abby's arms.

CHAPTER 39

Los Angeles, California

Leigh's eyelids flickered faintly, struggling to keep the light out. A door banged open somewhere above her and she heard a man speak.

"See, I told you. If I didn't call you, I'd have girl in my bathroom, door locked."

"Alright sir, we'll take it from here. Just clear the way so we can get her out to the ambulance."

Her eyes shot open, and she sat bolt upright, caught just in time by an ambulance attendant.

"Hold on sweetheart. Don't try getting up…"

Leigh felt her head swim, and swayed over.

"Do you have epilepsy? Did you take any drugs? Anything you can tell us now before we get you to the ambulance?" the attendant asked, helping to slide her onto a gurney she hadn't even seen them bring in.

She whispered something, faintly. It was too low for either of them to hear, and sent a long glob of black goo from her mouth and down her cheek.

Out of the corner of her eye, she could see the ambulance attendants exchange looks.

CHAPTER 40

Los Angeles, California

One of the intruders spun around, distracted enough by Theo's cry to drop Abby against the corner of the wall. Her head cracked loudly against it, and her shirt tore to reveal bruises already beginning to form. Nonetheless, she attempted to get up again.

Hunter continued to race toward the other, attempting to catch him by surprise. "Theo, take him!" he yelled, not bothering to see if Theo obeyed.

The other assailant turned as Hunter spoke, catching him between the ribs with an axe. The crunch of bone was all anyone present could hear, ribs bending and crushing under the sharp, shrill weight of the swing. Shards of the already pointed bone shot in all directions from the impact, his chest and side collapsing almost before he even hit the ground and becoming concave. One of the shards found its way into his lung, while another found his liver and immediately began to expel mass amounts of blood. He gasped for air, the colour draining from his face as he turned to face his attacker.

The man's face was emotionless and sterile as he brought up the axe again.

Theo watched, transfixed as Hunter's eyes widened, and with his last burst of strength, drove the blade through his murderer's gut.

"*No!*" Abby yelled, racing toward Hunter as Theo's opponent moved to take advantage of his shock. She grabbed a blade out of Theo's sack and raised it above her head, swinging it toward the man. Her eyes started to glow bright orange as she brought the blade down, and a fiery explosion burst through the blade.

Her hair coiled about her body, shaking in the force of the explosion as it traveled down the sharp metal of the blade and passed through him. Fire seemed to explode forth from every facet of his being, as if it were leaking right from him like magma.

The light blinded Theo, and he brought his hand up to his eyes to shield them from the glow.

There was silence.

Slowly, Theo lowered his hand, eyes meeting Abby's. She looked hollow as she stared at the charred carcass in front of her, blade still clutched in her hand. A circle of ash and scorch marks spread out from the corpse, stopping just feet away from her and Theo.

Carefully, Theo got up, moving toward Hunter's still body. He knelt next to him, brushing hair out of the dead boy's eyes. They were open, unmoving and dull, his lips parted and stiff.

Theo let his hands glide over Hunter's eyes, closing them gently. He barely knew the person laying before him, yet felt he deserved some respect, despite how things had seemed.

"I don't think I loved him…" Abby whispered, eyes not turning toward the body. Theo turned to look at her, but she continued to stare at the pile of ash in front of her.

"I don't think any of us had the chance," Theo replied, moving toward her. She stood before he had the chance to reach her, and silently walked into the hall.

The El Dorado sat in a gas station parking lot, backseat filled with luggage, front seats filled by two blonde men, appearing as father and son.

"She gonna be ok?" Theo asked, peering toward the rear of the gas station, where the washrooms were located.

Victor turned and stared at the female washroom door, squinting at it as though he could do-the-math on it as well. "I have no idea. Two boyfriends dead in one year, not an easy thing to come back from… and what was that?"

"What?"

Victor shot him a look. "What she did. What was that?"

"Admins at PHI called in Kinetic Disruption… but they really had no fucking clue what it was. It only happens when she's in proximity to someone as they die. That last breath triggers it, somehow. They didn't know why."

"They just… told you this?"

Theo smirked at him. "For the line of work they were in, they weren't too smart about dealing with telepathy."

"Mm. Well, no more secrets from you, alright? Got anything else you need to share?"

Theo narrowed his eyes.

Darkness. Like ink, swirling on marble and glistening in the night. Bubbling beneath the surface, something raw and un-tapped... Slowly eating away...

"Nothing I can think of," he answered, clucking softly.

They sat in silence for a moment, Theo tapping the rhythm to an unknown beat on his legs.

"You know it's going to be a while before we stop tonight, right?" Victor said, motioning toward the station again. "You might want to follow her lead and take a pee break."

"What do you mean?"

"Just before Abby called me last night, I got another call. We're not going to Arizona quite yet."

"Where are we going then?"

"Idaho," Victor replied curtly, gripping the wheel tightly.

"Another one of us misfits?"

He turned and locked eyes with the younger man, his face deadly serious. "Not even close."

CHAPTER 41

Northton, Idaho

"Will everyone just calm down?" Sheriff Martin Lane pleaded, rapping his palm against the rackety old desk he sat behind. All around him the collective swell of the town's voices remained, rising and falling in a mad drone that could be heard and understood by no one.

The Northton Town Hall was small and humid in the best of circumstances, which this meeting certainly was not. In generations past it had been the type of one room chapel that seemed to have been cloned into every small town in America, with its white panel siding and hastily placed steeple. There were no stained glass windows, just regular rectangular ones that had the hinges to open, yet for some reason could not. There were alternating theories regarding whether they had rusted or been painted shut or both, but either way there was no reprieve from the hot fall air as nearly three hundred of the town's residents piled in and around pews that were meant to fit no more than fifty.

Martin sighed and took off his hat, running his fingers through his thin reddish hair as he looked out over a crowd of people talking to anyone and everyone at once, each with their own plan and opinion and facts about one thing: the disappearance of Mary Crane.

"We should fucking kill him!" shouted Lief Ridge-wick, loud enough for everyone to hear from the middle of the assembled masses. "I always told you about that boy, always!"

"Why hasn't there been an Amber alert? He could have taken her anywhere by now!"

"Boy's not that smart... dumb as rocks he is, always was. Can't expect anything else from someone like that."

"Lord knows what he could have done by now."

"Been days! He could come after my child next!"

Martin let his gaze float over the crowd, aimlessly focusing on different faces. Jessica Hart was standing on her seat to the far left, yelling something angrily at Jackson Cooper on the right. Her curled hair was frizzled and bayful with the heat, her chest covered with sweat and threatening to lunge right out of her blouse every time she shook her finger at him. Her mouth was moving in wild, unrestrained syllables but Martin could not hear one word above the crowd, making her look like one of those actors in the poorly dubbed films imported from Japan.

Jackson Cooper was yelling back, his string of barely coherent curses clearly audible through his gaping maw of missing teeth. Martin had heard these words from Jackson many times before, and it elicited a headache between his eyes that he'd begun to associate with the man. It seemed that every Sunday Jackson was in his office, lecturing him about the 'illegalities' and 'indecencies' that had gone on in Northton that week. He was loving this now... the abduction of Mary Crane had left him feeling vindicated, as though he'd been right all along and yet been ignored.

His gaze finally fell to the front row, where an old woman sat in the pew directly in front of his desk, cooling her sweat drenched face with a folding fan. The moisture rolling down her wrinkled and dragged out face made it seem as though she was melting. She let out a loud huff and adjusted herself on the stubborn wooden pew, looking around at the people near her with annoyed glares as though it was beneath her to be there. As though she'd been forced to come, rather than just shown up. She had and been the first person seated, but that was neither here nor there.

She was Betty Clambers, and the fan she was using in a futile effort to beat the heat identified her almost as much as her face. It was white with goldenrod trim all around its border and a plastic clasp that was larger than usual to make it manageable for fingers that may not be as mobile as they had once been. When unfolded at its fullest it displayed a pattern of a snow white dove with an arrangement of flowers clasped in its beak, some of them falling out and floating around in majestic beauty. It was given to the eldest woman in the community, a title that at the age of ninety-six Betty had held for the last four years straight. There was another ornament like it, a silver cane, given to the eldest man that was currently owned by Leland Power of Elm street. He'd received the honour the last two years, the both of them standing side-by-side on stage at the town's summer festival and smiling gruesome smiles as local reporters snapped their pictures.

infinity

She let out another huff, then quickened her pace with the fan. "In my day this never would have gone on so long," she said, to no one in particular. "Sheriff Davis would have had this solved by lunch time."

"Okay!" Martin said, his voice full of exasperation. Several people in the first few rows stopped talking to pay attention, but the rest didn't even hear him. He kept talking anyway, hoping that as his voice travelled they would get the hint. "What we need here is organization, people. We have a missing girl and a suspect of her abduction, and we need to --"

"Suspect?!" came a loud voice from the crowd. This time everyone was quiet, all heads turning to look as a single man pushed his way from the middle of the crowd to the front. He was balding with thin glasses and a large jaw, and even the few people in town who didn't know him recognized him as Lucas Crane, Mary's father. His face was red with rage, the flesh on his neck shaking like the water of a kettle about to boil over. "Suspect? Why are we still calling that freak a suspect? We know he did it!"

There were a few hollers of adulation from the crowd.

Martin began to look over them, his face going slack as Lucas parted the people between them.

"Everyone knows he did it! We've known for years! Ever since that child has been here he's been nothing but trouble!"

More hollers, accompanied by several empowered fists being thrust into the air.

"He tried the same thing with Allison Grimm's daughter a few years back, remember?"

More yells, and nods of recognition.

"And Clarence, remember that thing at the fair last year? Remember when he come at Robert Junior's son two years ago? Damn near broke the child's nose!"

Martin moved his chair back from the table, watching as the crowd changed from hundreds of competing sounds into one unified, clear intentioned voice.

"The Miller's caught him in their back yard!" screamed a voice from the crowd.

"Was watching me from the trees last spring!"

"Always caused trouble!"

"Scared the life out of my daughter last Halloween!"

"We have to find him!" Lucas bellowed above them, raging through their voice like a brush fire through dry kindling. "We have to save my daughter! My Mary!"

The crowd continued to hoot and holler and talk amongst themselves. The only one who wasn't joining was Betty Clambers, looking from side to side at the increasingly angry people and waving herself with her vintage fan.

Martin again looked out over them, watching the air above them become thick and wavy as the humidity and the body heat formed a scorching combination, raising the blood pressure of everyone in the room and only making things worse. As he watched them he saw them become one voice, as though something were controlling or possessing them all, bending their rage and their hate into a weapon to be directed wherever the mob saw fit. Slowly he felt himself give up, and he nodded.

From the back of the chapel, just up from the double wooden doors, Victor shook his head in dismay.

To his right, Theo and Chad looked over the crowd from left to right and then back again, taking in all the people as they shouted and screamed angrily. Chad's eyes were wide and his lips were pulled tight, his long hair matted against his forehead with moisture. Theo's brow was so taut that it had formed a thick stitch between his eyes that looked very painful. His eyes were bloodshot and the skin on his face looked white.

To his left, Abby stared out over the accumulated crowd and cringed. She wasn't a weak woman, especially not in the last few weeks, but something about all those people made her feel things she hadn't since Jasper had died. It was close to fear, but that didn't describe it in and of itself. There was awe too... as though she were looking at something terrible and divine all at once. The wrath of God made flesh. She turned to Victor, taking a step closer to him as she did. "What is this?" she asked finally, her voice a hushed whisper.

"This is the reason you three need each other," he growled between clenched teeth, lowering his eyes at the crowd.

$$\infty$$

She ran so fast that the evergreen branches around her seemed to blur into one long green brush, sometimes whipping at her tender pink flesh with such ferocity that it sliced open in tiny, stinging paper cuts. So fast that even when her mud-covered bare feet tripped on a rock or slipped on a stray sliver of moss she did not fall, the opposing leg zipping out all on its own and finding earth before she could do much more than duck. So fast that the nervous sweat on her forehead ran backward instead of down, caught in the draft of hot air she created as she fled.

Mary Crane had never run so fast in her entire life. The adrenaline coursing through her made her heart slam like a jackhammer, her legs churning like pistons and feeling like rubber. She was beyond pain, beyond heat, beyond exhaustion. She ran as though it was all she knew how to do, as if she'd been doing it her entire life. For the briefest of instants, it occurred to her that she had. That life was not what we thought it was, that her existence had begun when her feet had hit the ground an hour ago and that everything that had come before it had been a dream her tortured mind had invented while on the run. This thought lasted only an instant though, like most she'd had in the last sixty minutes. Mostly, the only thing her conscious brain did was scream the constant, urgent order to flee.

There was very little of her supple pale flesh left visible below her knees. Most of it had been splashed with thick, gravelly mud, some of it now dry and some so fresh that it still sloughed off onto the branches that tore at her even now. A select few areas of her shins had been scraped and sliced by the foliage and itched like hell, one of the only things she could still feel below the waist. One of her toenails had been ripped out, blood spurting from it and mixing with the mud to create a malicious shit-brown hue. There was a chunk of flesh the size of a quarter missing from her ankle, so deep that her meat could be seen underneath.

Her face was decorated with small, razor-thin scrapes that stung fiercely when perspiration found them, but otherwise went unnoticed. Her hair was matted to her chubby, full cheeks, clinging to the blood and sweat as though they were glue. The only part of her face magically unobstructed were her eyes, wild and wide and blue. They were glossy with tears that blurred her vision even further, making it hard to tell the stones from the puddles or the dips from the hills.

Her blouse was in pieces throughout the trees, grasped by the greedy fingers of the forest. Her legs were bare, her lower half covered only by the slender panties that she'd had on when she had made her escape. Her rich, full lips curled as she strained her ears to hear something other than her own trek through the brush, for some sign that her flight was over.

Gathering her courage, she turned over her shoulder and peered through the gaggle of straw hair.

He was less than ten feet back, the sun and the leaves leaving odd patterns against his bald head. His yellow, jaundiced eyes were squinted into tiny slits against the trees, surrounded by folds of pink mush where a normal persons eyelids would have been. He was breathing so hard that his mouth was open, showing off a gaggled and twisted maw of teeth that seemed to point in every direction except straight. Each exhalation that escaped from between them sounded like steam escaping from the stack of an oncoming train, powering his every thrust forward. He moved like a cat, those two fingers and toes grasping each log and rock with amazing dexterity. He was so fast she wondered how he hadn't overtaken her yet.

She turned back toward the front, bobbed her head to avoid a large branch, and kept running.

CHAPTER 42

Northton, Idaho

Sun shone brightly through the orange and red leaves, making the day seem warmer still than it really was. A digital thermometer flashed 84.2°F on the Police Station sign, and Chad wiped the sweat off his brow as he looked at it angrily.

"I fucking hate small towns," he spat, peering out the windshield of the parked El Dorado. "All the people act as if state law doesn't exist. It's like a fucking lynch mob usurped all forms of leadership."

"You'd hate them more if you could hear their thoughts," Theo mumbled, rubbing his temples.

"What?"

"It's like one big hive. They all think the same, they hate the same. All I can see is red... and the face of that monster."

"Thing really looks that bad?" Chad asked, eyebrows raising.

"He reminds me of a guy I knew once. Was a burn victim, had doused himself in gasoline one night. After he healed up his skin was uneven and patchy. Imagine that, except with pointed teeth and inhuman looking eyes."

"So I take it they've never heard the phrase 'don't judge a book by its cover'?"

Theo's eyes locked with Chad's. "Definitely not."

Chad broke his gaze, staring at his hands. The silence was uncomfortable, yet still, he had to ask.

"Why'd the guy douse himself in gasoline?"

Theo smiled grimly. "He heard voices, too."

CHAPTER 43

Northton, Idaho

Abby had stripped down to a tank top, unbuckling the straps of her overalls so the top half fell at her waist. Her hair was pulled back and her skin was sticky.

She leaned against a wall and glanced at a few *Wanted* and *Missing Child* posters tacked up along the opposite wall of the Northton Police Station while she waited for Victor. Mary Crane's photo was there, as well as photo of the boy who'd taken her. The two were beside each other. Mary's picture, under a *Missing* heading, was a standard school photo. The other, under the *Wanted* heading, was a grainy image of the boy smiling, revealing pointed teeth. His photo, unlike Mary's, had obviously been cropped from a larger picture.

Abby pushed herself off the wall, moving in closer to the photo. It appeared someone else had been cropped out of the photo, someone he'd had his arm around. Her brow furrowed, and she spun quickly around to stalk toward Victor.

"Yes, I understand the Sheriff is busy right now, but

we need to speak to him regarding the case he's attempt-ing to build," Victor said to the receptionist. She was a fat whale of a woman, tottering on her small chair behind a glass panel and shaking her head.

"It can't be done, sir," she repeated in an accent so thick she might as well have had a mouthful of marbles. "The sheriff won't be seeing anyone today."

"Oh shut up, Agatha. Stop trying to stop people from bringing in more information," Martin Lane said, coming around a corner toward the desk. He glared at her a mo-ment, and she shied away quickly. Turning to Victor and Abby, he smiled. "Sorry about that folks. Why don't you follow me back to my office?"

"Every person in this town knows that damn boy is guilty," Agatha mumbled to herself, face going complete-ly red.

"Agatha, do your job, or you won't have one!" Mar-tin bellowed at her, escorting Abby and Victor through a door. When they were in his office and the door was closed, he let out a long sigh and then walked around to his desk. "Sorry about her. Most the town would prefer if we didn't take the time to go through the proper chan-nels."

"It's a small town thing," Victor nodded, though did not look to approve or disapprove. "I get it."

"They don't seem to realize it's just plain good for when we take the boy to trial," Martin apologized, wip-ing sweat from the back of his neck with a handkerchief. "Now, what can I do for you folks?"

"We'd like a little information on the boy. Got a couple questions that need answering, if you're up for it," Victor grumbled.

Martin seemed taken aback. "I can try, but there's nothing I can really tell you other than what is public knowledge."

"Alright, then let's start with the basics. What actual evidence do you have that this was indeed a kidnaping, and that the boy was even involved?" Victor asked, staring the Sheriff straight in the eye.

"The girl went missing, she's a good kid. No fight with her parents, no enemies. The boy's been seen going around her place a bunch lately, skulking around outside. We have several witnesses to that. One lady called a sighting in around half an hour before the girl was reported missing."

"So what you're saying is you're relying on a few eye witnesses and no hard evidence? No sign of forced entry and nothing to prove conclusively that he was even there?" Abby said, glowering.

"Well, you have to understand... this boy is well known to be a troublemaker. He got kicked out a few years ago from his foster parent's home because he was stirring the pot. I never thought he was really a bad kid, but I guess every man has their breaking point."

Abby nodded slowly, her gaze going past Sheriff Martin and to the peg board lining the wall behind him. She squinted, again looking over even more copies of the Missing and Wanted posters. The same two of Mary and her abductor looked back at her, matching her gaze even through the grain and wear.

"Sounds unverifiable," Victor frowned, looking Martin up and down. "I was at the town meeting. There's not one person there I wouldn't call biased. Not one person that wouldn't say they saw something even if they didn't, if it meant stringing him up."

"You saying you think he doesn't have her?" Martin asked, leaning forward and raising an eyebrow.

"I'm sure he does," Victor huffed, rubbing the bridge of his nose. "It's the system I'm sick of."

"Who did you say you were with again?" he asked, taking out a pen and paper.

"I'm --"

"Where'd that photo come from?" Abby piped, still staring at the disfigured boy on the *Wanted* sign.

The sheriff sat for a moment rubbing his temples, then mumbled a reply.

"What was that?" Victor asked, eyebrows drawn together.

"It was submitted," he repeated, lowering his arm.

Victor looked from Martin to Abby and then back again.

"It looks cropped," she continued, raising her finger into her own vision, as though she could mark where she was pointing with a laser pointer. "See? The way the pixels are all grainy. Wrong size too, dimensions. It's perfectly square, pictures are rectangular."

Victor followed her gaze, tilting his head to one side.

"And this means...?" Martin sighed, turning only briefly to look at the photo.

"There's a Ferris Wheel in the background there... and his arm's stuck out." She raised her own to try and match the angle, and ended up putting it directly onto Victor's shoulder. "He's with someone there."

"Who submitted that photo?" Victor asked, finally joining her train of thought and pointing to it. "Who else is in it?"

Martin sighed. "Lucas Crane. And I don't know."

Victor smiled. "Now that is a funny thing," he said, then picked himself up out of his chair. "Let's go, Abby."

CHAPTER 44

Northton, Idaho

Lucas stared into the forest, his eyes shining with hatred as the branches danced about in front of him, mocking him with their rhythmic, circular swirls. Between them he could see bits of motion and colour, but whenever he turned to focus on them they were gone. It was as though the trees themselves were taunting him the way schoolyard bullies would taunt, dangling his prize in front of him before making it disappear with one smooth flick of the wrist the second he tried to grab it.

He turned down his head and closed his eyes, whispering softly to himself. In the evening light, his face became shadowed and dark until almost none of his features were visible. When he opened his eyes again, the whites seemed stark and bright. Slowly, he turned around to face the people behind him.

Almost twenty men and women were assembled there at the mouth of the forest, many with the same thick boots and all with the same horrid look of determination. Several drank coffee from paper cups, brought in a large thermos, while others just stood there.

"He told us to have patience," Lucas spoke finally, his voice low at first and then rising with every word spoken. "He told us to wait!"

Several men yelled their encouragement.

"Well I say we can't wait! I say *every minute* that that beast spends with my daughter is a horror! That it must be stopped!"

Again, more yells. They echoed all the way down the block.

Lucas marched forward through the crowd until he found his truck, large and red and splashed with the same mud that his feet were now sinking into. Grunting, he slid the latch off the back with a mechanical whine, then thrust it open. It bounced twice on its old springs as he reached in and grabbed a red plastic gas can.

A few of the faces in the crowd lost their guile, but not as many as should have.

Lucas turned and marched back toward the wood.

"Hey, Luc," Pete said in a low voice, reaching out and grabbing his arm as he walked past. "What're you doin'?"

Lucas pulled his arm away, turning around and taking the last few steps in odd sideways slides so that he could still talk to his friend without being deterred from his goal. "Spent some time up in Montana as a boy," he said, reaching the forests edge.

Pete squinted and shrugged.

Lucas kicked over the can and let its contents chug their way out into the brush. He reached deep into his jeans pocket and pulled out an aging bronze butane lighter, flicking the flint and watching the flame grow in front of him. "Learned all I ever needed about smoking out a fox."

He dropped the lighter into the brush.

The flame spread quickly, bathing his face in light.

Smoke filled the muggy air, creating a thick blanket that hung over the El Dorado, impeding Victor's view of the road. Theo shifted nervously in the passenger's seat, ash drifting across the windshield, falling gently and smearing with each pass of the wiper blades. His brow creased as he stared out into the darkness.

Abby's eyes traced the outline of his face, dancing over the little bit of him she could see from the backseat. He looked liked a cornered animal, his breathing shallow and quick. His eyes seemed far away, and she wondered what could be on his mind.

"Any idea what we're heading into?" Victor asked him in a low voice, the purr of the engine almost obliterating his speech.

"They set the forest on fire. If we don't get to the kids soon, they'll be dead," Theo mumbled, trying to look out onto the road. "This place is just that fucking crazy."

"It's a town full of hicks," Chad piped up. "You really thought they'd account for the fact that fires spread fast this time of year? All they want to do is barbeque their children."

The road bent suddenly, and the car jolted to the left. The El Dorado sped down over an embankment, sending the occupants forward in their seats.

"Fuck!" Chad yelped, bracing himself against the frame of the car. It spun out of control, sending them toward a tall evergreen tree. Victor flung the wheel to the left, sending them away from danger, and down an overgrown trail way.

"Okay, we're going to die now," Abby squeaked, gripping the sides of her seat as branches whipped along the windows.

Victor pulled around a bend, and suddenly the car arrived along the side of the road once more.

"Everyone out," he said, opening his door. "I'm not taking the car any further into that shit. From here on in we're on foot."

∞

Mary felt her feet fly out from under her, slipping on dry, mossy rock. She winced as the pain hit her, breath leaving her lungs as the wind was knocked from her. Her blonde hair was matted and tangled, the broken off leaves and twigs creating a sick halo around her head. A sob escaped her lips as the breath returned to her body. She had lost him in the smoke, and was unsure how long it would be before he found her again. She couldn't bear to think about it. She just needed to find a safe place before the smoke engulfed her for good.

She picked herself up, limping slightly as blood trickled down her left calf. She set her jaw firmly, bracing against the pain as she took each step. The smoke was slightly thinner here, and she thought she could make out where she was.

She pushed through the forest cautiously, watching her footing as best she could, finally finding a large tree with its roots upturned. Underneath it was still moist with rot, despite the heat wave blowing toward it. She poked at it with her foot, seeing how far it went down. Getting down on her knees, she began to pull away clumps of dirt. When she was satisfied, she lowered her legs below.

Feeling the scraping of small, sharp rocks against her hips, she slid herself under the tree. The smoke was more bearable the lower she was, and the cool dirt protected her from the worst of the firestorm. She wondered when the fire brigade would come, or if they even would. So many times, there would be forest fires like this in the area and the trucks wouldn't get to it before the forest was entirely decimated.

The cracking of a tree rang out over the sound of flames. Mary cringed, wondering how close the fire had come. Peeking her head out from the hole, her eyes met the sight of bare, misshapen feet. Each had only two toes in the front, with a third misshapen one coming out the back.

He had found her.

CHAPTER 45

Northton, Idaho

Abby stopped by an old birch tree, using the mangled arm of its branch to hold herself up. There was a weight on her chest that she couldn't explain, dragging down into her stomach like a stone. Her free hand went to her gut and pressed hard, the edges of her mouth trying to run their way off of her face.

"Are you okay?" Theo asked, stepping up behind her and putting a soft hand on her shoulder.

She turned and shot him a look filled with daggers, her eyes wet and stingy from the smoke all around them. "Like you don't already know."

He removed his hand and watched her walk away, wiping a long tendril of sweat from his brow as the heat began to eat at him.

Victor stepped up behind him, his footfalls remarkably silent given his size and the rough terrain. He didn't speak, just watched Abby trudge ahead as Chad passed them, his eyes scanning the hazy brush for any sign of movement.

"She's still upset about Hunter," Theo sighed.

"She's not, really. She thinks she is, but she isn't."

Theo squinted at him. "You didn't really like him, did you?"

"I'm sorry he's dead."

"That's not what I asked."

Victor turned slightly so that he could see Theo clearly, but did not respond.

"What *was* it about him?"

"Can't you find that out for yourself?" he said, a smirk on the side of his face that Theo couldn't pin as genuine or snarly or anything in between.

"I don't think you thought very much of..." he paused, reaching out and grabbing the same branch Abby had to keep himself from falling.

Victor reached out and wrapped out of his massive arms around him, holding him up around the chest. "What is it?" he snapped.

"Mnng," Theo grunted, his nostrils curling and the flesh atop his nose folding onto itself.

Victor looked up into the forest, his brow furrowed and his eyes becoming small. He stayed that way for almost a minute, eyes fluttering from one direction to the next. "You're getting something, aren't you?"

"Got it in the car, too," he managed to say, bringing a hand up to massage the bridge of his nose yet still not quite able to stand.

"It's the mob. All those thoughts the same... the voice it creates must be deafening."

"It's not them. It's something different. Something strange. Not quite a thought, but close."

He got up, taking several deep breaths to compose himself.

"Have you gotten it before?" Victor pressed, flicking his hair out of his eyes.

"Yes," Theo said coldly, watching as Abby and Chad disappeared into the brush. "But it's not something I expected to find here."

CHAPTER 46

Northton, Idaho

Lucas slammed the heel of his boot down against a branch, cracking it in two and sending the top half spinning into the brush from the sheer momentum of it. It spun wildly, flicking splinters this way and that before disappearing into the smoke.

A thick layer of sweat covered his entire face, culminating in several large beads on his upper lip. He turned back as Jackson Cooper passed by him, both their breaths as haggard and steely as the others, like two animals exchanging respectful grunts between the trees.

The crowd behind him had grown somehow, or maybe it just seemed that way. With smoke seeming to billow from every nook in every tree, it surrounded them until all he could see were trucks and smoke and them.

His wife Kim was there, and he was glad she was.

Sheriff Martin was there too, forcing his way through over a sprouting sapling and nearly breaking it in two. He looked up solemnly and met Lucas's eyes, the both of them holding it for a long moment.

The smoke was both terrifying and exhilarating at the same time, like the exhaust of their march through the forest. Lucas took in a deep breath, in through his nose and out through his mouth, feeling the heat as it filled him and worked its way throughout his body. He could feel the molten pockets of air like cinders now, grazing against the lining of his throat and lungs and making his rage something tactile. Something real. Something hot.

"Over here!" Jackson yelled, his voice as loud and booming as when he gave sermons each Columbus Day. "I've found something!"

Lucas raced for where Jackson's darkened silhouette stood against the smoke, looking as though someone had cut his shape out of gray construction paper and let the excess fall away, revealing the blackness and void behind it. It was a black hole, and Lucas ran toward it faster than gravity could have possibly carried him. Behind him, he heard the footfalls of the crowd become faster, more energized than they had been since they started their expedition... almost falling in unison now, their combined might forming a clapping thunder that echoed off the rocks and the trees and then back again until they became never-ending.

Jackson came into view, his right arm partially obscured as it held back a particularly massive branch of evergreen to reveal a large, open field of wild grass.

It was tall, at least chest height, and seemed to go on forever. The trees on the other side of it looked like miniatures from here, small enough to be flicked aside with an errant breath. The grass was the pale brown of death that happened every fall, so dry that it would become kindling within seconds when the fire finally reached it.

"I don't see it," Lucas said finally, eyes scanning the horizon line frantically. "I don't understand."

"There," Jackson whispered, his arm extending between them and pointing straight down the middle of the field.

Lucas's eyes squinted for a moment, straining to see, before widening dramatically when he finally saw what Jackson had been talking about.

Toward the center of the field, almost obscured by the grass, was a large, smooth rock. Except it moved, ever so slightly. Up and down, back and forth. Up and down, back and forth. It was a soft ashen colour with small flecks of white, making it seem like bloodless dead flesh. There were rivets going up the center of it, bumps in its otherwise smooth surface placed in even intervals all the way up to... its head.

It wasn't always visible, only slightly at the end of its up-down momentum, but it was there. The small bump of a bald head, obscured almost completely by what was now unmistakable as its back. Like one of those unfathomable magic-eye pictures, once he saw it for what it was he couldn't *not* see it.

Lucas's face drew out, losing all emotion. His eyes became dead and transfixed, almost crossing themselves as he stepped forward and into the field.

"Luc?" Jackson asked, voice still hushed and whispered. "Luc? Lucas?"

There was a small dip in the topsoil between him and the field and he walked over it, falling like someone who had stepped off a building to their death. He landed on both feet and kept walking without missing a beat, not noticing let alone stumbling.

The creature's smooth backside still moved, up and down. Up and down.

Suddenly, the rage returned.

"Hey!" Lucas yelled, though when it came out it wasn't so much a word as a bellow. His voice sounded like it was bubbling over and his face was as red as fox fur. The rest of the crowd began to filter from the trees as though they were coming from them, like demons of the forest itself.

The creature turned, and if ever it had been in doubt what it was, it was gone now. Its eyes were slanted, almond shaped slits in the center of its head. Without the benefit of any nose to speak of they looked to be suspended there, their grip to its skull tenuous at best. They were jaundiced and bright and soulless and although pupilless, Lucas could tell that they were locked onto him.

Mary's head appeared just below it, her eyes wide with fear. Even from this faraway vantage point, Lucas could see that they were welled with tears.

"You son of a bitch," Lucas said, mostly to himself. He started to run toward them, faster than he had in years. Faster than he would have thought a man his age were capable of before today. "You *son of a bitch*!" he bellowed, cheeks flapping wildly with the vibration of the sound.

Its eyes went wide and it leaped off of Mary, its long, slender legs taking it up and out so far and so fast that it was almost like it was flying, the way a daddy longlegs or a gazelle might leap. When it landed it was nearly ten feet from Mary and vanished beneath the grass line, popping its head back up a moment later.

Seeing Lucas still plowing its way toward it, it now finally noticed the crowd that had become mob behind him
that was also storming forward. Eyes wide with fright, it
turned toward the opposite side of the clearing and started to run.

That was when Abby shot herself into the clearing,
followed less than a moment later by Victor, Theo and
Chad.

"Sweet Jesus," she gasped, her eyes falling over the
crowd.

Theo winced, bringing his hand to his temple again.

"Something's wrong," Chad said simply. "It shouldn't
be this way."

The creature turned, only to find that the crowd had
caught up to Lucas. They were almost on top of it now, a
human wave of anger and retribution and death, a thousand stomping feet ready and willing to come down upon
him at a moments notice.

"I'll kill you for this!" Lucas screamed from somewhere in its middle, and the voice seemed to come from
the crowd itself. As though each person was a cell in a
larger, much more dangerous organism that had been
given form by their combined hatred. "I'm going to fucking kill you!"

Theo's nose began to bleed.

"Come on!" Victor yelled, stepping in front of the others and starting toward the creature. "Come on!"

They started to run, Theo dripping blood into the
grass with each step.

The creature looked back over its emaciated shoulder
as they started toward it too, and seemed to let out a long,

shaking sigh before it fell to its knees. The tall grass tick-led the sides of its high cheekbones and it closed its eyes as Lucas Crane and a mob of dozens descended upon it.

Lucas snatched a small bat from someone, drawing it back and then shooting its base forward with every ounce of drive he'd accumulated.

"No!" Mary screamed, thrusting her body on the crea-ture and knocking it to the ground.

Lucas stopped, his eyes wide and the colour finally draining from his cheeks.

She stared up at him, her golden hair in front of her eyes and tumbling down over the creature's chest and head, like a woven shield. Her eyes burned intensely, burring smouldering holes into her father's head.

Victor stopped, squinting. The others stepped a little closer, Abby finally coming to a halt only a few feet from where Mary lay.

"What are you doing?" Lucas hissed, thrusting a fin-ger to one side. "Get off of him! What do you think you're doing?"

"Go away, Daddy!" she spat, her sweet lips curling in disgust. She was breathing hard now, as was the thing she guarded. All its ribs were visible with each frantic inhala-tion, expanding and contracting so quickly that it almost seemed to be playing in double-time.

"Go away? What do you mean, go away?" The colour was returning now, first pink and then that venomous, verbose crimson. "He took you away!"

"He didn't take me, I ran away!" she spat, sitting up finally and aiming her typically smooth but currently jag-ged body at her father. "Ran away from you."

"That is interesting," Victor whispered, tilting his head and looking at the creature again. There was fear in its face, he could see it now. He didn't know how he hadn't before. It came off of it in waves, almost more powerfully than the sum of the mobs rage had been.

"Didn't do the math on that one?" Chad commented, unable to resist turning to smirk at Victor.

"The odds are always one hundred per cent after the fact," he whispered, eyes glued to the scene before them.

"You wouldn't let me see him! Wouldn't let me near him, wouldn't even let me outside!" Mary screamed, rage building in her own cheeks now.

"Him?" Lucas huffed, his bat falling to his side. "Why would you want to see *him*?"

"I love him, Daddy."

CHAPTER 47

Northton, Idaho

A hush fell over the crowd.

Theo's nose stopped bleeding.

Abby watched as the last dribble of blood found its way to his chin and dripped to the grass. "Is it over?"

He squinted, his gaze moving from one end of the crowd to the other. "For some of them."

"The rage isn't gone," Victor corrected, moving up to stand between them. "Just dispersed. That same thing took the anger out of some of them but tripled it in others."

"Love it?" Lucas said, Kim stepping up behind him. "You love it?"

"It's not an it, it's a him. He's my boyfriend."

"He's brainwashed you."

"He's been my boyfriend for *five months*," Mary screamed, her fists clenched to either side of her. Behind her, her boyfriend stood up and placed two of its massive fingers on her shoulder in support. She brought her own to it and they interlocked gently.

Lucas locked eyes with it for a long moment, finally dropping the bat to the ground.

"Finally," Chad sighed, smiling.

"Shit," Theo and Victor said, almost simultaneously.

Lucas drove his fist forward, slamming into the creatures mouth with such force that it knocked one of those long, jagged teeth into the grass.

It fell backward, its fingers jolting from around Mary's as blood gushed from its unprotected nostrils in large globs. It wasn't as thick or as meaty as blood should have been, coming out like fruit punch that had been left in the sun for too long and splashing onto the ground. Before it could even get up, Lucas was on top of it.

"No!" Mary screamed, diving for her father. Jackson grabbed her by the arm and pulled her back into the crowd, and suddenly there were more hands restraining her. Hands that apart would have been nothing, but together formed the links of chains that were unbreakable. Still she fought against them, biting and punching and kicking and screaming. "Daddy, stop!"

Lief Ridgewick stepped forward with a tire iron he'd grabbed from the back of his car before they'd set out and paced around Lucas and the creature as Lucas pulled back a fourth time and slammed it in the face, this time hitting its eye so hard that it almost popped out. Snarling, Lief saw his opening and brought the iron up high with both hands, bringing it down on the creature's knee in one crunching blow.

The sound was remarkable, even with all the noise of the crowd. A horrible sound only recognizable to people who'd witnessed buildings collapse and ten car pileups, moist and sudden and fierce.

The kneecap shattered as though it had been made of glass.

The creature howled, but only for a moment before Lucas's fist connected with its lower jaw.

"Don't just stand there, get in there!" Victor bellowed, his voice as intense as a Viking battle cry and just as potent. The other three joined him as he slammed into Lief's mid-section, thrusting him to the ground. The tire iron came loose and vanished in the field as Victor's fist drew back, connecting with the larger man's nose an instant later.

Lief Ridgewick would not wake up for thirty-two hours.

Victor stood, tossing his head back. His hair threw itself to either side of his head and his bushy eyebrows narrowed, turning his eyes into needlepoints that scanned the crowd instantly. He reached out with two massive paws, slamming onto a man's back and hauling him out of the crowd, connecting his fist with the man's neck and then moving on to the next without even noting where and how he fell.

Abby pulled Kim Crane free and threw her to the ground, glaring at her in disgust for a moment before moving on. A man tried to grab her by both shoulders but she shrugged out of it, dipping down and pushing her whole body into his central plexus ramrod straight. He fell back into the crowd like a singer diving into a mosh pit, punching at her back and kidneys as he went down.

Chad was on the ground almost immediately, beneath a big bruiser with a goatee and tattoos going all the way down both arms. The man drew back and smiled, then brought both hands down quickly and savagely.

He thrust himself to the side and the man kept going, both hands connecting with a large stone that had been underneath him. There was a snap and a splurge of blood as the man bellowed in pain, folding over and clutching his useless hands to his chest.

"Sure," Chad shrugged, moving into the crowd. "Why not?"

Theo had already taken down three of them, his feet moving back and forth like a boxers. There was a blade in his hand but it was reversed, the sharp edge riding down his forearm so that only the butt of the handle stuck out between the fingers of his clenched fist. Every punch he made was like a symphony of motion, his opponents telegraphing their attacks to him before they made them. Two more descended upon him now, the butt of his sword connecting with the first's adam's apple and his knee drove into the second's gullet. They went down together, one atop the other.

Lucas thrashed out again, the face he was driving his knuckles into now hardly more than a maw of ashen flesh and thin, stringy blood.

"Stop it!" Mary cried, finally forcing herself free as more and more of the people around her left to stop Victor and Theo. She turned to her mother, who was watching her husband with shock and horror on her lips. "Stop this!"

Kim rose to her feet and both women moved toward Lucas, their teeth clench and ready, adrenaline streaming to their muscles and giving them strength.

Mary grabbed him by the right shoulder and hauled

him back off of her boyfriend.

He pushed her off of him and onto the ground, her hips skidding and scraping along the gravel.

"Lucas!" Kim yelled, as she reached out to grab at his other shoulder.

He drew back his arm to punch Mary, so blind by rage and blood he didn't even see her. Didn't recognize her.

His elbow connected with Kim's nose, driving her back in a spurt of blood and mucus.

She went down soundlessly, her head slamming against the same sharp rock that Chad had lay on a moment before.

Lucas turned, the rage gone now and replaced by fear.

The creature sat up, its yellow eyes pleading as it reached out its two-fingered hands toward the woman.

Mary's bottom lip began to quiver, her eyes finally overflowing with massive, salty tears. "Momma?"

Abby's eyes burned bright orange.

"No..." she whispered to herself, clutching both her hands together at her chest as she bent over in pain. She felt like her body were collapsing in on itself, along with everything around her. As if her chest had become the center of gravity for the entire universe and everyone and everything around her were being drawn in. Even the air around her seemed to bend and twist, the way it did on a hot day when the sun beat off the pavement.

"Shit," Theo gasped, eyes growing wide as he ducked down below the grass. "Fire in the hole!"

All at once her arms spread out, a wave of flame and heat erupting from her and spreading outward quickly with enough force to push everyone around her back. The grass caught fire and burnt itself all the way down to its roots, turning the entire field into nothing but smouldering soot. The mob blew back, dispersing them and sending all of them onto their backs as the shockwave shot past them. For a moment they were in hell's furnace, the air around them so dry that it sucked the air straight from their lungs.

CHAPTER 48

Northton, Idaho

Victor stood up first, the tips of his hair singed. He let out a deep breath as he looked over the sea of unconscious bodies around him.

Mary lay against her mother's bosom, sobbing uncontrollably as her father stood off to one side. His mouth was open and his eyes were wide, tears coming from them freely.

The Sheriff got to his feet and stepped over to the creature, handcuffs in hand and dangling.

"What the hell do you think you're doing?" Chad groaned, getting to his feet. His eyebrows were burnt but could still glower, and did readily at the town cop.

"Relax," Martin said, his voice harsh and hoarse, like someone who'd downed an entire gallon of scalding hot coffee. "It's over. I'm taking him in for his own protection until we get everything sorted out..."

The creature stiffened, backing away from the man fearfully.

"... if that's okay with you, son?"

It stared at him suspiciously for a long moment, then nodded and brought its wrists forward.

Theo rose to his feet groaning, steam billowing off his backside. Rubbing the bridge of his nose for a moment, he surveyed the situation as the officer cuffed the creature's first hand. Suddenly, his eyes went wide and he turned to Chad and Victor: "He's lying."

Snarling, Sheriff Martin took his revolver from his holster and brought the muzzle down flush with the creature's temple, already putting first pressure on the trigger. He didn't gloat or speak or spit, just pulled back the hammer and loaded the bullet into the chamber.

"No!" Chad screamed, leaping for the gun with both hands outstretched.

He fell short, tumbling into the burnt soil.

-BANG.-

Everything was silent, even the sounds of the forest.

Chad turned and looked up, almost afraid to see but still needing to. His face was covered in dust and the skin on his forehead had been ripped clean.

Mary's hands covered her face and she began to cry again, more than she ever had before.

Theo's eyes went wide and he turned back to Victor.

Victor stood in the background, a grin on his face mostly hidden by his scruff, looking almost exactly the same as he had when he'd met Chad and Koy in Janelle's diner. "Now, what do you suppose are the chances of that happening?"

The creature looked up at the Sheriff, his eyes wide with fright and confusion.

The Sheriff took the gun away from its temple and

looked at it, smoke trailing out both ends. He turned it around and examined the barrel, seeing the dull copper glint of the end of the bullet that was stuck there.

He turned back to the crowd, and the last thing he saw that day was Mary Crane's fist coming toward his face.

Martin fell toward the boy and he scuttled out of the way, allowing the Sheriff to fall face first into the dirt and stay there.

Theo, Abby and Chad walked over to Victor and watched as Mary collapsed to her knees, the adrenaline finally wearing off and grief returning to her in massive, heaving clumps. She started to cry, to scream out wailing moans as her tears soaked the ruined earth around her, her entire body going limp.

Abby watched, remembering full well what grief like that felt like and still unable to accurately put it into words.

Lucas went to his daughter, wrapping his arms around her and starting to wail himself. She resisted at first, but only at first, driving her nose into the warm nuzzle of her father's neck and continuing to cry.

The creature stood off to the side and watched, staring at the ruin helplessly.

Both Mary and Lucas turned up and noticed him at the same time, his already disfigured face even more so after the abuse he'd taken. Solemnly, Lucas motioned him over.

He collapsed into their embrace and let out a long, mournful wail.

The three of them stayed there like that, huddled into one another, drawing strength from one another for a long time as the others watched, unsure of what if anything to say.

"What's your name son?" Lucas said after a long time, swallowing his pride along with his tears and mucus.

"Maximus," the boy said, holding both father and daughter close. "My name is Jean-Claude Maximus."

EPILOGUE

Somewhere, Arizona

Abby Fisher stared out at the bright light of morning, the sun making bursts of light off of the dew covered grass. The sky was noticeably clearer than it had been mere hours ago when she had first assumed her current position, leaning against the rail of her balcony. In that moment she was as still as the trees, and inside her waters were calm and placid.

A small smile crept over the sides of her face.

At that moment, she felt younger than she ever had. At twenty-two, she wasn't old by any means, but even now she felt as if this was the beginning of a new life. As though she'd spent everything up until now asleep and was finally and fully awake. An energy coursed through her that she could not shake, washing over her like the sun's rays.

Below her, Jean-Claude and Mary lay on the floor of the gazebo, their feet the only thing really visible, entwined in each other. She couldn't really hear what they were saying, but knew they were talking. And somehow, although she couldn't see their faces, she knew they were smiling.

Chad and Karen were just a few yards away, pushing Koy on a swing set. She was laughing wildly, looking back over her tiny shoulder at the highest point of each arch, as if to make sure he was still there. Chad smiled in a way he hadn't in years as Karen watched, her hand gently massaging the doughy flesh of his shoulder. She laughed along with Koy and after a moment they took her out of the swing. Chad threw her into the air and caught her, tickling her and making what had been a infectious giggle turn into an all out roar.

Abby giggled too. Behind her, Theo looked up from the bed and smirked, then turned his attention back to his laptop.

On the far east corner of the grounds, Abby caught sight of Victor. He was standing next to the fresh grave of Hunter Mason, a man whom she had thought was the answer to questions she'd been asking for a year and now realized... realized that the answering of questions was overrated.

"It's the question itself... that's what makes life great," she said to herself, rubbing her hands up and down her arms.

Theo looked up again. "What was that?"

"Nothing," she hummed happily. "You know, they say there are only two questions in life that really matter: where do I come from, and what am I going to do next?"

He nodded. "What are we going to do next?"

"I'm not sure," she admitted, laughing. She leaned forward onto the rail with both arms, letting the warm Arizona wind sweep up and into her hair and felt alive. She watched as Victor bowed his head and clasped his arms in front of himself silently. "But I can't wait to find out."

Victor stared down at the simple, inelegant headstone of Hunter Mason and frowned, clasping his cell phone tight to his ear.

"It is a shame, I suppose... well I know *you* liked him, but I never much did. Uh-huh. Uh-huh. Well I guess all teachers have some little place in their hearts for their first graduate," he paused, turning back to watch Chad and Karen roll Koy around in the freshly cut grass. He noticed Abby in her bedroom window out of the corner of his eye and smiled at her.

"I don't think we'll be needing him though... you should have seen them Tash, they were incredible. The three of them, the way they worked... the way it just *clicked*... it was like fate," he paused, listened to the voice on the other end of the line, and beamed. "I guess I *haven't* talked like that in a while, have I? Yeah, yeah I think he'd be proud too."

He smiled, running a hand through his thick blonde hair and casting a watchful eye over those he'd assembled as he listened.

"No, I think I'll let them enjoy themselves tonight. Relax, enjoy it.

"They've got a lot of work ahead of them tomorrow."

ENGEN TIMELINE

With over twenty novels spread over three different series by many different authors, the Engen Universe of titles is growing every day and into genres we couldn't have imagined! From the original ten book *Black Womb* thriller series, its crime novel sequel series *Xander Drew*, our flagship adventure title *Infinity*, or single-novels like *Jacobi Street* or *light|dark*, there's something in the Engen Universe for everyone with more books by more authors on the way soon!

...But how do the events relate to one another, chronologically? While some astute readers have guessed at the potential timeline (some accurately, some not), we're going to finally set the question of the Engen Timeline to rest.

Turn the page for an up-to-date guide of the ever-widening world of Engen, featuring the works of Ellen Curtis, Andrea Hackett, Ali House, Sarah Thompson, Jay Paulin, and Matthew LeDrew!

In the 10 Years Prior Black September

"Reptilia" by Matthew LeDrew
published in *light | dark*.
Danger descends on a small secluded town in the
form of a deadly virus with fantastic and terrible
side-effects. Can a small group of doctors escape
alive?

Compendium by Ellen Curtis
Three short stories forming the basis for the
Engen Universe's ties to suspense, genetic
engeneering, and the supernatural. Features the
stories "The Tourniquet Revival," "Falling into
Fire" and "At Midnight, the Dawn."

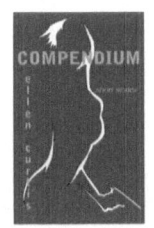

"The Theogony" by Matthew LeDrew
published in *light | dark*.
A tale of young Theo Flaherty of the *Infinity* series
and his time admitted against his will to the Black
Springs hospital, where he learns to paint, and
seeks out his father.

Black September

"Revving Engen" by Matthew LeDrew
published in *light | dark*.
A direct lead-in to both *Infinity* and *Black Womb*,
Tasha travels to Coral Beach, Maine on a hot tip
about a recently discovered young man with
incredible abilities.

Infinity by Ellen Curtis & Matthew LeDrew
Faced with a destiny he's uncertain of, the
enigmatic Victor must bring together four unique
people with very special abilities… or face the
tasks ahead alone. Guaranteed to excite!

Black Womb by Matthew LeDrew
Fifteen years ago, something happened in Coral Beach, Maine that resulted in the present death of a seventeen-year-old boy. Now four high-school students must try to solve the mystery... before the killer picks them off.

Jacobi Street by Matthew LeDrew
When a mysterious painting shows up at an art gallery he works at, Bob must work with Eddie and Sloan to track down its sinister origins and convince the people living on Jacobi Street of them, before its too late!

Transformations in Pain by Matthew LeDrew
When two girls are assaulted and one is hospitalized, the residents of Coral Beach must put their shared tragedies behind them and stop the man responsible, as well as unlock the secrets behind the true nature of the Womb...

Year One: October

Smoke and Mirrors by Matthew LeDrew
The approaching trial of Genblade brings closure to the people of Coral Beach, until people start showing up dead in the same manner they did when he was at large.

"Scarlett" by Andrea Hackett
published in *light\dark*.
Introducing Scarlett, the slightly damaged hunter on a mission to save others from the monsters from her past.

"The Inevitable" by Ali House
published in *The Lightbulb Forest*
A young woman must contend with the emergence of a frightening new power alongside the emotional high of a first date.

The Tourniquet Reprisal by Curtis & LeDrew
A man lives in Atlanta, Georgia that people don't talk about, but everyone knows he's there. He arrived a year ago and turned a gaggle of uneducated youth into something new, something to fear.

Roulette by Matthew LeDrew
As the teen suicide rate in Coral Beach starts to climb astronomically fast, Xander travels to Los Angeles to fight his most terrifying adversary yet… and learns that the only thing worse than looking for release… is finding it.

Year One: November

Exodus of Angels by Curtis & LeDrew
Victor's enigmatic past is illuminated when Jaycee accompanies him to visit a new friend in the paliative care ward of the Black Springs hospital, where Theo also happens to be searching for a cure for Leigh.

Ghosts of the Past by Matthew LeDrew
Coral Beach faces its most awesome threat when one of Engen's past mistakes is unleashed upon the unsuspecting populous. Friends and enemies unite to fight a common enemy… but will even that be enough?

Touch Your Nose by Matthew LeDrew
Simon Monk must infiltrate the San Fransico
branch of Shane Industries, a massive company
with deep ties to the Engen Universe. Where do
his true loyalties lie? And can he get out without
causing harm?

Ignorance is Bliss by Matthew LeDrew
After being set through the ringer one too many
times, Xander decides that his life with Julie
needs a little more attention… which is bad news
because a new villain has come to town with his
sights set on Adam Genblade.

"Gristle While You Work" by Jay Paulin
published in *light|dark*.
A short story centering around the rise of a new,
and possibly cannibalistic, serial killer in the
Engen Universe.

Becoming by Matthew LeDrew
For months Xander Drew has been doing his
level best to keep the streets of Coral Beach clean,
which means it's time for the forces of darkness to
strike back… all at once.

Inner Child by Matthew LeDrew
Julie is hospitalized with life-threatening wounds
to both body and soul. But the real threat comes
from the hospital walls themselves, as a demonic
presence makes itself known to Xander and his
friends.

End of Year One

Gang War by Matthew LeDrew
The Tees, a homicidal gang of evil men, has finally been taken down by Xander Drew. But his victory is short lived, as retired Tees are mysteriously killed. With a town of suspects, anyone can be the culprit… including one of their own.

Chains by Matthew LeDrew
Sociopath Derek Smith has been freed from prison and is praying on the weak; and none are weaker than August Styles: a pregnant girl with Down Syndrome who has run away from home.

"Omega" by Ellen Curtis
published in *light|dark*.
A sinister division of Engen begins a series of experiments on pregnant women in a fashion eerily similar to those that created the original Black Womb project.

The Long Road by Matthew LeDrew
Xander meets the American people — and realizes that the world is harsh and wicked, but can also be soft and gentle, even loving. Xander Drew comes of age on the road, and sets his new direction.

Year Two

Cinders by Matthew LeDrew
Detective Horton enters a violent and dangerous world he didn't know existed beneath the veneer of order and structure that he has based his entire deductive method around.

Sinister Intent by Matthew LeDrew
One of the killers Detective Horton could not catch has resurfaced: a serial killer who flaunts his sinister intent in front of the Los Angeles Police Department, making it so that no one is safe.

Faith by Matthew LeDrew
Xander's mysterious and troublesome past returns to haunt him on the streets of Los Angeles; a place where even more people can get caught in the crossfire of the games of death and deceit that makes up his life.

Flickers in the Night by Matthew LeDrew
Lisa Rowdan is hunted by her haunting -- and powerful -- ex-boyfriend Ryan through a lonely city street. Can she escape him?
One of over twenty great sprine-tingling short stories!

Family Values by Matthew LeDrew
Xander and his new friends Crowley, Lisa, and Tim investigate a series of kidnappings and murders that stretch back decades, all of which have the same similar twist: victims being found after years of being missing.

The Future

"Remers" by Sarah Thompson
published in *light | dark*.
In the not-too-distant future of the Engen Universe, young athletes are the targets of a scouting program to create the next stage of super soldier with cybernetic enhancements.

ON SALE NOW FROM ENGEN BOOKS

HEED THE CALL

After a heated fight at sea between twins Ben and Alex, Ben vanishes from their boat without a sound or even a ripple in the water. Unwavering in his dedication to find his brother, Alex begins the adventure of a lifetime armed only with the help of a local girl named Meg and his own mysterious musical abilities... the key to which, and to the mysteries that surround him, may be tied to the alluring song of the dangerous girl he finds among the ocean's frothing waves.

about the authors

Ellen Curtis is a writer and web tv personality born and raised in St. Johns, Newfoundland; whose aptitude for the written word began at a young age, when she began writing short stories, poetry, lyrics and novellas.

She was 'discovered' at a Sci-Fi on the Rock writing panel in 2008, and her first collection of stories, *Compendium*, was published just over a year later in October 2009.

Since then she has risen to become one of Engen's lead authors, working on high-profile projects such as the *Infinity* series of adventure novels, as well as continuing her own endeavours.

In her spare time she enjoys reading, art, music and spending time near the ocean.

Matthew LeDrew studied Journalism at College of the North Atlantic in Stephenville, Newfoundland and has worked with Transcontinental Publishing, as well as the student-youth magazine *The Troubador*.

He has written six other novels for Engen Books: *Black Womb*, *Transformations in Pain*, *Smoke and Mirrors*, *Roulette*, *Ghosts of the Past* and *Ignorance is Bliss*.

He lives in St. Johns, Newfoundland.